ERROR OF JUDGEMENT

A cold case ignites in this gripping murder mystery

JOHN DEAN

THE
BOOK
FOLKS

Paperback published by The Book Folks

London, 2019

© John Dean

ISBN 978-1-0956-2769-3

www.thebookfolks.com

Error of Judgement is the sixth stand-alone novel in a series of British murder mysteries featuring Detective Chief Inspector Jack Harris. Look out for the others: Dead Hill, The Vixen's Scream, To Die Alone, To Honour the Dead and Thou Shalt Kill.

Chapter one

Strapped into his aeroplane seat, Passenger Eleven stared wordlessly ahead. There was little sound in the gloom, which was punctuated only by a pale glimmer of light that filtered through to where he was sitting. The only noises were murmured voices that echoed from afar but seemed to be getting louder and closer. Not that Passenger Eleven reacted to their approach. He had not reacted to anything for a long time. Instead, he sat and waited to be discovered and for his secret to be revealed.

* * *

The mountain rescue team picked their way steadily across the moorland, their boots squelching through the damp heather as they walked beneath North Pennines skies that were rapidly darkening and laden with rain. The blue sky of a few hours previously had vanished and the ribbons of cloud were now thickening, as the gathering winter wind blew in the threat of yet more downpours.

It was midday and the seven-strong team and two dogs had been walking for a couple of hours. From time to time, one or another of their number would glance uneasily upwards; they all knew that bad weather was forecast, and the last thing they wanted was to have to bring the injured girl down hillsides that had been turned even more slick and treacherous by rain.

Although they walked with steady and sure feet, a legacy of years spent traversing the northern hills, there was an urgency to their movements. The emergency call had come in shortly after ten that morning from a panicky young man. He said that he and his girlfriend had been camping out on the hills, and that she had slipped while they were picking their way along a narrow ridge. She had slid a couple of hundred metres down a steep wooded slope, striking her head several times against rocks on the way down, before coming to a juddering halt against a fallen tree trunk.

Now, said the boyfriend, she was unable to move, was in great pain and was drifting in and out of consciousness. She was also growing increasingly cold and his attempts to get her to answer his questions had met with little success; she was struggling to even recall her name. Shortly after the call, the mobile phone's signal went dead and repeated attempts to call him back had failed.

After assembling at their hut on the edge of the market town of Levton Bridge, the team had driven to the nearest parking place to the site of the incident, left the Land Rovers and started up into the hills, walking in the easy silence that came from many years of working together. Besides, words were not required; each one of them appreciated the gravity of the situation. Hypothermia was concerning enough but head injuries changed everything, and the team knew that every minute was precious. Lives had been lost on the hills before and anything that delayed the rescuers' progress increased the chance of another tragedy. Instinctively, their pace quickened as they neared the ridge.

Shortly before noon, they reached the place where the woman had slipped. Team leader Bob Crowther, a north country man born and bred, and a veteran of many rescues, stood and stared down at the thinly-wooded hillside for a few moments, struggling to pick anything out. He fished a pair of binoculars out of his bag and, after a couple of minutes of further scanning, gave a grunt of satisfaction and pointed at a scrap of blue half way down the slope, barely visible in among the trees.

'There,' he said. Crowther handed the glasses to the man standing next to him.

Detective Chief Inspector Jack Harris took a few seconds to pick it out then nodded and handed the glasses back.

'Nice spot,' said the detective, who had been a member of the team since his return to work in the area several years previously.

Harris slipped his bag off his shoulders and glanced down at his dogs, who were looking up at him expectantly.

'Sit,' he said.

Scoot and Archie, mongrels both, did as they were told.

'Good boys,' said Harris. The inspector took a handful of snacks from his coat pocket and threw them to the animals. He looked down the slope again. 'Looks like she fell quite a way, Bob. She's lucky not to have got herself killed.'

'Much good may it do her unless we can get her out fast.' Crowther frowned as a blast of cold air swept across the ridge. 'She's been lying there for the best part of three hours.'

He looked back at the way they had come, staring across the expanse of bleak moorland stretching into the distance, the clouds continuing to darken and the wind gathering in strength.

'They certainly picked a fine place to do it,' he said. 'We're well away from the main trails. I can't remember the last time we had a call-out here.'

'No, I don't often get this far over either,' said Harris. 'I'm not sure that anyone does.'

The inspector glanced down at the expanse of loose shale that lay between the ridge and the trees.

'And getting her up this way will be awkward,' he said. 'Any ideas how we tackle it, Bob?'

'Too risky to bring her up the slope. Hang on.' Crowther pointed further down the hill. 'See half way down? On the tree line? That looks like a stream, doesn't it? Maybe we go in there and follow it through. Could give us a clean run to get her out.'

'Could do,' said Harris. 'When's the chopper back from its other job?'

'Within an hour, apparently. If we can get her to that patch of open ground, they should be able to winch her up.' Crowther turned to his team, who were already unpacking their gear. 'Be careful down there, guys. It looks like it's going to be very slippery.'

'Yes, Dad,' said one of them.

'Are we there yet?' said another.

Everyone laughed and Crowther grinned at Harris.

'No fucking respect,' he said.

Within twenty minutes, the team had scrabbled their way down across the shale earth and waded through the bracken until they reached the stream, its waters already swollen by winter rains. Following its path through the woodland, the rescuers repeatedly slipped on the wet stones.

'This is treacherous,' said Harris as he grabbed onto an overhanging branch to avoid falling.

Crowther nodded, his mind already considering other options. After a few minutes, they turned away from the crash of the water and moved carefully up the slope through the gloom until they came upon the young couple. The woman was propped up against the tree trunk, her eyes closed and her face twisted in pain. Her boyfriend greeted their arrival with a look of relief.

'Boy, am I glad to see you,' he said.

'Tom Hawley, is it?' said Crowther.

'That's me. I thought you maybe couldn't find us.'

'We tried ringing you.'

'Annie's phone died,' said Hawley. 'Low battery. And I forgot to bring mine.'

Bob Crowther said nothing but the rest of the team knew what he was thinking. Following a series of similar incidents over the previous month, he had been interviewed on local radio, urging walkers to ensure that they were properly prepared when taking to the hills. Jack Harris noticed him shake his head and shot him a rueful look. Crowther crouched down next to the girl.

'Annie, can you hear me?' he said in a loud voice.

She nodded feebly.

'Where does it hurt?' he asked.

'My head.' Her voice was little more than a croak. She ran a hand over her forehead. 'Like something's broken.'

'Well, we'll soon have you out of this,' said Crowther. 'First, we'll get you checked out by one of our medics. She'll give you something for the pain.'

He gestured to one of the team to attend to the girl, stepped a few metres away and indicated for Harris and team deputy Mike Ganton, another veteran North Country man, to join him.

'I don't like the look of this,' said Crowther in a low voice. 'There's a good chance she's got a fractured skull – if the boyfriend is right about her hitting her head on a rock, that is.'

'Definitely a job for the chopper then,' said Ganton.

'I guess,' said Crowther. He frowned.

'Something bugging you, Bob?' asked Harris.

'I'd have expected her to be much paler given what she's been through.' Crowther glanced back at the girl and pursed his lips. 'There's quite a bit of colour in her cheeks.'

'Yeah, I thought the same thing,' said Harris.

'What's more,' said Crowther, 'she's nowhere near as cold as I thought she'd be.'

'We can't take any risks, though,' said Ganton. 'I mean, if she has got a fractured skull, or maybe internal bleeding, we have to get her out of here pretty damn quick. And I don't fancy tackling the stream again, Bob. We only need to go over once when we're carrying the stretcher...' He did not finish the sentence. He did not need to.

'Yeah, I know,' said Crowther. 'Which is why I want you two to scout another way out.'

Tom Hawley, who had been edging closer and listening to their conversation, walked over.

'I thought down through the trees and out that way before you got here,' he said. He pointed down the slope. 'It looks a bit drier.'

Crowther nodded.

'It seems to be our best option,' he said. 'Check it out will you, guys?'

'Will do,' said Harris.

The two men started walking and Hawley made as if to accompany them.

'Stay here,' said Harris. 'We don't want two of you getting injured.'

'I'll be alright.'

'It wasn't a request,' said Harris curtly.

Hawley looked as if he was about to remonstrate but something about the inspector's tone of voice made him think better of the idea. Ten minutes later, as the two men and the dogs were working their way downwards, holding onto trees to keep their balance as they repeatedly slipped on the steep slope, Archie barked and ran off into the gloom, followed by an excited Scoot.

'Here, boys!' shouted Harris, but the dogs did not respond. 'Bloody things! Perfectly obedient until they get distracted.'

'Yeah, mine are the same,' said Ganton. 'One of them chased a couple of cyclists down the lane for the best part of a mile yesterday.'

'Probably deserved it,' grunted Harris.

'They *were* wearing bright green Lycra.'

'There you are then,' said Harris. 'You get what you deserve in this life.'

Ganton chuckled.

'Is that what they call community policing?' he said.

After a couple of minutes walking as quickly as they dared, the men could hear the dogs growling. Emerging into the half-light of a small clearing, they came to a halt and stared in open-mouthed amazement at what had scared the animals. Archie and Scout were crouched low, fangs bared, ears pinned back, eyes narrowed, as they looked at the skeletal remains of a man strapped into an upright aircraft seat, wearing the tattered shreds of what looked like it had once been a dark suit.

After taking a few moments to regain his composure, Mike Ganton walked up to the body and leaned over to peer at the seat number, worn with age but still just about decipherable. He rubbed it to make the figures clearer.

'Well, well, well,' he said. 'If it isn't Passenger Eleven. Never thought we'd find him. Not after all this time.'

'Everything turns up if you give it enough time,' said Harris. The inspector instinctively reached out to lightly touch the bony cheek. It was smooth and showed little sign of weathering. Harris frowned.

'Is it worth trying CPR?' said Ganton.

Harris gave a slight smile. 'Probably not,' he said. 'Mind, I'm no medical expert.'

'I guess this puts paid to all the conspiracy theories then.'

'You'll never get rid of conspiracy theories,' said Harris. He stepped back and surveyed the body with a thoughtful expression on his face. 'In fact, I have this awful feeling that they are about to start up again.'

'Bloody hell,' said a voice. 'Not what you expect to find in a place like this.'

They turned to see Tom Hawley approaching through the trees.

'What are you doing here?' snapped Harris. 'I told you to stay with the others.'

'Sorry. Wanted to check if I was right about the way out. I'm worried about Annie.' Hawley walked up to the skeleton. 'That's amazing.'

Harris noticed that he was holding a smartphone in his hand.

'If you're thinking about filming it, you can forget it,' said the inspector.

'I told you, the battery's dead.'

'So will you be if you film it,' muttered Harris under his breath.

Chapter two

'So, tell me more about Passenger Eleven,' said Detective Sergeant Matty Gallagher. He was standing in the clearing and watching the forensics officers as they busied themselves around the skeleton in its aeroplane seat. 'I've only heard bits. What exactly do we know about this John Graydon character?'

'Not as much as we'd like,' said Harris. The inspector turned up his hood as water dripped ever faster off the trees. The predicted bad weather had arrived and rain was sweeping hard and cold across the moors.

'But we know that he was a fraudster?'

'That much we can say for certain, yes.'

The officers stood in silence for a few moments and watched the forensics team at work. The detectives were very different men: Jack Harris was born and bred in the valley, at home on the hills, strong-jawed, and had thick brown hair without a hint of grey; Matty Gallagher was a decade younger, smaller, stocky, had black hair starting to thin, and was a man, some said, with the appearance of a monk. A Londoner who had moved to the area so that his wife could be nearer her elderly parents, the sergeant was a long way from his comfort zone as he stood shivering on the wooded slope. He looked up nervously as a particularly strong gust of wind led to a groaning and creaking from the trees.

'Will the chopper be able to get back up here to take the body off the hill?' he asked.

'Yeah, the weather should hold long enough.'

'You sure?'

'Trust me,' said Harris. 'I've seen it much worse than this.'

'There's a reassuring thought,' grunted Gallagher as the trees creaked in the wind again. 'And what about us? How are we going to get back down?'

'We'll have a nice stroll in the country.'

'I was afraid you might say that,' said Gallagher with a sigh. There were many times when he missed London and this was one of them. He looked over towards Passenger Eleven. 'Why did the plane crash then?'

Before the inspector could reply, Bob Crowther and Mike Ganton appeared through the trees.

'I heard the chopper going down the hill,' said Harris as they approached. 'Did the girl get away OK?'

'She did,' said Crowther.

'Will she be alright?' asked Gallagher.

'She seemed a little better when we loaded her into the chopper.' Crowther frowned. 'Much better than I might have expected, in fact.'

'Still not sure about it?' asked Harris.

'No, there's something not quite right about this. I would have expected a few more injuries for someone who had fallen that far. All she had was a few bumps, bruises, and scratches. Not even any blood.'

'I guess some people are just born lucky,' said Gallagher. 'A bloke I knew won the Lottery three times. Mind you, he wasn't that lucky. I lifted him for buying heroin with it.'

For a moment, it looked like the inspector was going to say something but he thought better of it and stayed silent. Crowther glanced over to the man in the aircraft seat.

'I take it you want us to hang around for when the chopper comes back?' he said.

Harris nodded and Crowther gestured to the forensics officers.

'They'll have to be quick,' he said. 'The pilot reckons we're running out of time with the weather closing in.'

'He'll be ready,' said Harris. 'Matty was just asking what happened when the plane came down.'

'Hell of a night that was.' Crowther shook his head at the memory. 'Twenty years ago, but it's like it happened yesterday. I had not long joined mountain rescue. It was one of my first jobs.'

'It was just before I joined up,' said Ganton. 'Me and Shel were having dinner at my folks' place when Dad rushed in and said that a plane had gone down and that they had been called out. We didn't see him for three days.'

He was silent for a moment and the others stayed quiet, sensing that he was struggling with the emotion of the memories; his father had recently died.

'Dad must have seen some terrible things that night,' said Ganton eventually. 'He always told us about his rescues but he never talked about that one. I asked him about it once, years later, but he said it was best I did not know. I swear he was crying. The only time I'd seen that happen.'

'I never really talked about it either,' said Crowther. 'Not even to Maureen. Couldn't seem to find the words. Not sure there *are* the words.'

'Were you there?' asked Gallagher, looking at Harris.

'It happened when I was away with the army. I tell you, I have never felt particularly comfortable flying and what happened here was one of the reasons.'

'One?' asked Gallagher.

Harris did not elaborate on his comment.

'Where had the plane come from?' asked Gallagher. 'Somewhere in Scotland, wasn't it?'

'Prestwick Airport,' said Harris. 'Flying to Manchester. John Graydon was a businessman – or he claimed to be, anyway – and he'd chartered it to take a group of Scottish investors to see a derelict site that he wanted to develop. Paid for the wives and girlfriends as well. It was a proper junket.'

The atmosphere in the Astra Galaxy twin-engined executive jet was jovial as the lights went off in the cabin and the aircraft slowly taxied through the drizzle into its position for take-off at Prestwick Airport. Outside, the runway spotlights shone brightly in the gathering darkness of a late afternoon in winter, reflecting off the glistening tarmac. Once the plane had left the ground, it climbed steadily through the cloud before banking as it turned onto its southbound heading.

The 'fasten seatbelt' signs were extinguished, the cabin lights came on again and Passenger Eleven went to work. Time to do what he did best. Schmoozing. He stood up and let his eyes roam the cabin, particularly focusing on the besuited businessmen – no ties, as requested in the invitation. He gestured with the slightest flick of a finger to the stewardess at the far end of the cabin.

'Champagne all round, I think,' he said loudly.

A cheer went up from the passengers and one of the businessmen rubbed his hands in anticipation and looked cheerily at the busty blonde sitting next to him. She returned the smile and reached out to touch his hand. Passenger Eleven noticed the gesture and smiled as well. Candy from babies, he thought. It's just all too easy.

'Graydon had booked them into a posh hotel in the city centre,' said Harris. 'The best rooms, a slap-up meal, free drinks and a night at the casino with money in their back pockets.'

'Expensive,' said Gallagher.

'And all paid for by the good old British taxpayer, Matty lad. This was Blair's Britain. New Labour loved mixing with entrepreneurs and there was a lot of public cash being invested in bringing derelict sites back to life. And Manchester had acres of them to go at.'

'New Labour liked Graydon, I take it?'

'The money was there for the taking if you blew in the right ears,' said Harris. 'He had secured enough cash to persuade a number of private investors that it might be worth supporting his idea for the new business park. He was promising massive returns, apparently.'

'But it was dodgy?'

'Yeah, what the investors didn't know was that the Fraud Squad in Manchester had started an investigation into him a few weeks earlier. They'd heard a whisper that he was creaming money off for himself. They weren't even convinced that the plan for the business park was real.'

'Did he know he was under investigation?' asked Gallagher. The sergeant took another uneasy look up through the trees as a particularly strong burst of rain lashed the hill and the wind shrieked.

'No one's quite sure. Maybe he did, maybe he didn't. The Fraud Squad had certainly planned to arrest him when he landed at Manchester.'

'But the plane crashed.'

'But the plane crashed.'

'Does anyone know why?'

The final streaks of afternoon light had long since faded as the aircraft continued to head across the North Pennines on the short flight to Manchester. There was a party atmosphere in the cabin as Passenger Eleven went from seat to seat, being charming to the women, swapping banter with the men and continually prompting the stewardess to top up his guests' glasses.

In the cockpit, Captain Raymond Malahide, a veteran pilot who had worked for the charter company for a number of years, stared ahead into the darkness, noting with concern the thickening fog. He listened to the increasing sounds of hilarity from the cabin and smiled ruefully at his co-pilot.

'At least someone's having a good time,' he said.

'I'm not surprised, the amount of champagne that they brought on board.' The co-pilot looked anxiously at the control panel. 'The altimeter's playing up again, Ray. You want to turn back?'

'We'll get it looked at when we reach Manchester. We'll be there in half an hour.'

'Could be something serious.'

'It's not the first time it's done it. You know what the bosses are like about us turning back.' Malahide glanced out of the side window and frowned. 'Mind, I'd like to a have a visual in all this fog.'

The altimeter juddered again and the co-pilot looked over at Malahide.

'We really should put down,' he said.

Malahide hesitated.

'Ray,' said the co-pilot, more insistent this time.

Malahide sighed.

'OK, OK,' he said. 'Let's see if we can divert to...'

He gave a terrified scream as the fog thinned and the shadowy shape of a hill loomed into view ahead of them. Malahide grabbed for the controls and wrenched the plane into a steep climb, its engines screaming in protest, but it was too late and the aircraft clipped the ridge.

'The official inquiry decided that it was pilot error,' said Crowther. He glanced at Harris. 'That's right, isn't it?'

'It is, yes,' said the inspector. 'The report said that Malahide should have listened to his co-pilot. The investigators reckoned they lost track of where they were, which is why they hit Hobb's Point.'

After the collision, the plane continued to climb steeply for the best part of a minute with her engines still screaming as Ray Malahide battled desperately with the controls. In the cabin, passengers cried out in terror as they were thrown about. One man was lying unconscious on the floor, blood pouring from a gaping wound caused when an overhead locker burst open and smashed into his head. The man who had rubbed his hands in anticipation was

14

slumped in his seat, his eyes lifeless and with a large hole in his chest. Beside him, his girlfriend stared at him in uncomprehending horror, seemingly unaware of the blood staining her white blouse as it poured from her own injuries.

'Help him!' she cried, looking round wildly for help. 'Help him!'

She did not seem to realise that all of them had but seconds to live. Neither did the stewardess. Recovering her composure as the aircraft began to level out, she ran along the aisle.

'Seatbelts on,' she cried to those who were still able to hear their words. 'Put your seatbelts on!'

Which was when she glanced out of the window and saw that the night sky was illuminated by tendrils of flame. It was the last thing she ever saw. It was the last thing any of them ever saw.

'One of the fuel tanks had ruptured after the plane hit the ridge,' said Ganton, taking up the story. 'A piece of shrapnel or something. Without that, they might just have made it. There was an explosion and the plane broke into several pieces. A shepherd was the only person to see what happened and he described a fireball falling from the sky.'

'How many died?' asked Gallagher quietly.

'Eleven passengers and three crew.'

'No survivors?'

Crowther looked over to the skeleton in the aircraft seat.

'Not now,' he said.

Again, it looked as if Harris was going to say something. Again, he stayed silent.

'Most of the wreckage landed on the moors above Caltwith,' said Crowther. He waved a hand. 'But it was strewn all over the place. As were the bodies.'

He fell silent at the memory, recalling horrors he had tried to suppress for two decades. Once more, Ganton took up the story.

'There were kids bunking off school the next day to try and find bits of wreckage,' he said. 'They got chased off by the police but they couldn't stop everyone half-inching stuff.'

'That was the trouble,' said Harris. He fished a bar of chocolate out of his coat pocket and started unwrapping it. 'The black box recorder only confirmed that the pilots knew they had a problem with the altimeter but it didn't tell the investigators what had caused it. Their best guess was a wiring fault but the final report admitted that the investigators were not helped by the fact that so many bits were missing.'

'Including the altimeter,' said Ganton. 'It's probably sitting in someone's bedroom gathering dust.'

'Or out here somewhere,' said Crowther. He gestured in the direction of the moor. 'Bits still keep turning up. A couple of holidaymakers found a champagne bottle out this way last year. Unbroken, it was. Absolutely remarkable.'

One of the forensics officers walked over to where they were standing. She looked at Harris.

'We've done about as much as we can up here,' she said.

'You found anything interesting, Beth?' asked the inspector.

'Only what you'd expect. You don't have to be a genius to see that he's got multiple fractures.'

'So much for wearing your seatbelt,' said Gallagher. 'Clunk, click, eh?'

'His jokes don't get any better, do they?' said Beth with a slight smile.

'Afraid not,' said Harris. He did not mind; he had long since come to value the sergeant's ability to lighten sombre moods.

'So, can we get the chopper back up here then?' asked Harris. 'Is he ready to move?'

'The sooner the better,' said the forensics officer as another burst of rain lashed the hillside. 'I, for one, don't want to stay up here much longer.'

'I'll give them a call,' said Crowther. He took his mobile phone out of his trouser pocket, punched in a number and walked towards the edge of the clearing in search of a better reception. 'Tell Matty about the conspiracy theories, Hawk.'

'They started almost immediately,' said Harris. He took another bite of chocolate, ignoring the dogs as they watched him hopefully. 'It did not take long for word to leak out that John Graydon was under investigation and, because his body was the only one that had not been found, folks put two and two together and made five. Some people reckoned that he was never on the plane.'

'But surely he was identified when he went through security at the airport?' said Gallagher.

'Not that simple, Matty lad. He had a passport with his name and picture on it but John Graydon kept a low profile so no one actually knew what he looked like. There had never been any photos of him – nothing in the media, and the fraud squad didn't have anything. And since he was based in Manchester, none of the Scottish investors had actually met him. It was all fixed up through his office.'

Crowther rejoined them, shaking his head.

'This gets weirder and weirder,' he said. 'The chopper pilot says he has just dropped the girl and her boyfriend at the General and she walked into the hospital unaided. Seems I was wrong about a fractured skull.'

'There's a lot about this that does not add up,' said Harris. 'Is the chopper on its way back up here then?'

'It is, yeah. You OK if me and Mike get chummy ready for moving?'

'Sure,' said Harris.

Gallagher watched the two mountain rescue men head over to the skeleton, Crowther gesturing to another couple of his team to assist them.

'So how come John Graydon ended up here?' asked the sergeant. He peered into the darkening gloom of the

17

woodland. 'And how come he was never found before? I imagine there was a massive search, yeah?'

'Biggest in the history of the area. As for why he was not found, it is certainly true that a couple of the bodies fell out as the plane broke up in the air and were found away from the main crash site.' Harris watched as the mountain rescue team removed the skeleton from the seat and laid it reverentially onto a stretcher. 'But there's no way that they wouldn't have searched this wood.'

The inspector beckoned to the dogs.

'Come on, boys,' he said. 'It's going to be a long walk home.'

'Can't we call up an Uber?' asked Gallagher hopefully. 'My feet hurt.'

'City boy,' said Harris.

Chapter three

It was early evening by the time a weary and hungry Jack Harris returned to divisional headquarters in Levton Bridge. Guiding his mud-spattered white Land Rover up the hill, he cursed as he saw the ranks of journalists and television cameras gathered outside the Victorian building that housed the police station. Normally, the inspector would have parked at the front, even though he knew that it irritated the divisional commander – *because* he knew that it irritated him – but the journalists' presence made it impossible.

Speeding up, and ignoring the shouted attempts by reporters to attract his attention, he drove into the yard at the rear of the building, after which he made his way through the back door and up to his first-floor office. With relief, he slipped off his sodden boots, peeled off his coat, switched on the kettle and fed the dogs. Once he had settled down with his mug of tea, his desk phone rang. He sighed and picked it up.

'Harris,' he said.

'It's Leckie,' said a man's voice. 'Saw it on the news – it's on every channel. Figured you might need a bit of help.'

Graham Leckie, a uniformed constable with Greater Manchester Police, was one of the inspector's few close friends, the men having met when Harris worked for CID in the city. Even though Harris eventually returned home to Levton Bridge, they still talked on a regular basis because Leckie worked in force intelligence and the valley often witnessed crimes committed by criminals from outside its area.

'I might need help at that.' Harris tipped back in his chair, balancing precariously for a few seconds as he tried not to spill his mug of tea. There was a couple of moments' silence as he struggled to regain his balance.

'You nearly went over again, didn't you?' chuckled Leckie.

'You know me too well, Graham. I still get gyp from my shoulder after the last time. Are you up to date with what's happened here?'

'Just what I saw on Sky News. That you've finally found the elusive Mister Graydon.'

'So they tell me.'

'You're not sure?'

'Not entirely.'

'Who else could it be?' exclaimed Leckie. 'You've got a body, haven't you? One that fell out of an aeroplane? I mean, it's not Amelia Earhart, is it?'

'I've got a body, yes, Graham. As to whether or not it fell out of an aeroplane, I remain to be convinced. It is certainly designed to look that way.'

'Are you thinking it's a hoax?'

'Possibly. If I'm wrong, though, and it does turn out to be John Graydon, I take it you've got a lot of information about him?'

'You have no idea,' said Leckie. 'I popped down to records and we've got thirty-five boxes clogging up the place. Most of it is financial stuff, old-style paperwork, as you'd expect, but I am guessing you're not really interested in that. You just need to confirm his identity, I'm thinking?'

'For the inquest, yes. Out of interest, did he know that the Fraud Squad were after him?'

'No one is sure. Although his company handled large sums of money, it actually employed very few people. After the crash, the office closed down immediately, leaving a lot of unpaid bills and hacked-off creditors. The only employees the Fraud Squad tracked down were a secretary and some woman who did the payroll. Neither of them were much use.'

'Anyone else involved?' asked Harris.

'Graydon's right-hand men.' Harris heard the sound of fingers tapping on a keyboard. 'Edward Gough and the somewhat exotically named Perry St Martin. Exotic for Altrincham, anyway. A couple of smooth-talking hot-shots in their early twenties, by the sounds of it.'

'Anything more specific?'

'A few dodgy connections in Manchester's underworld, that's all. St Martin had previous for handling stolen goods and Gough did a bit of time as a juvenile.' More tapping. 'Couple of break-ins. Drugs-related.'

'I don't remember either of them,' said Harris.

'Not sure you would have. Strictly bottom feeders. Way below the level that you were looking at when you were here. Couple of wannabees, that's about the size of it.'

'Any idea what happened to them?' asked Harris.

'They had it on their toes after the plane went down. Word was they turned up in Spain. Just let me read through this.' Leckie did not speak for a few moments. 'Nope, looks like they have not been heard of since.'

'Probably changed their names.' Harris took a sip of tea. 'You got anything that might help me confirm that my skeleton is John Graydon?'

'Computer says no,' said Leckie, mimicking David Walliams.

There was silence at the other end.

'You really should buy a telly,' said Leckie. 'Ah, I'll tell you what we do have. A scan of the passenger list from Prestwick, which confirms that Graydon was booked on as Passenger Eleven. I'll e-mail it as an attachment. Oh, and you need to know that our fraud squad have recently re-opened the case.'

'Really?' Harris lowered his feet to the ground and leaned forward. 'You never told me that.'

'I didn't know until I started digging around this afternoon. They did it a few days ago.'

'Any idea why?'

'I am afraid not. All very hush-hush, apparently. The chief has got a bee in his bonnet about it and they've got a go-getter in charge of Fraud Squad now, Jenny Armannsson. Out to prove herself. You'd like her.'

'What do you mean?'

'You know what I mean, you dirty dog. Anyway, her lot reckon that Graydon may still be alive.'

'I'm sure they do. The conspiracy theories have been doing the rounds again what with the twentieth anniversary coming up.'

'Well, Fraud Squad had certainly heard enough to be intrigued,' said Leckie. 'I'll keep you in the loop.'

'Cheers,' said Harris. 'I haven't forgotten our fishing trip either. Suggest some dates when you send the document.'

'Will do,' said Leckie and the phone went dead.

As Harris replaced the receiver, a dark-haired woman walked into the office. Gillian Roberts was Levton Bridge's detective inspector, the organiser, a mother-of-two whose carefully-cultivated matronly demeanour masked a mind as sharp as they came. She surveyed his dishevelled appearance.

'Nice walk?' she said.

'Lovely.'

'Must have been.' Roberts sat down at the desk. 'You've tired young Matthew out. He's fast asleep in the squad room. Either that or he's dead. I suppose I should have checked.'

'Yeah, he looked like he was struggling towards the end,' said Harris. 'Did you get someone down to Roxham General to talk to the girl?'

'They should be there by now. You reckon that she and her boyfriend are in on it then?'

'In on something. Like I keep telling folks, our dead guy looks wrong for someone who's been thrown from an aeroplane.'

'Yes, but how do you know that?' asked Roberts.

'Take it from me, I just do.'

Before Harris could elaborate, a slim, balding uniformed officer walked into the office. Philip Curtis, the Divisional Commander, frowned as he noticed the inspector's muddy dogs slumbering beneath the radiator. Although he and Harris had worked hard to develop a good working relationship after a difficult start, the presence of the dogs at the police station remained one of their disagreements. However, Curtis knew that the animals were popular with the rest of the staff, so he said nothing. Harris noticed the commander's expression.

'They were the ones who found the body,' said the inspector helpfully.

'If you are hoping that will get them into my good books, you can think again,' said Curtis. He sat down at the desk. 'In fact, this is the last thing we need. Bloody Pantomime. Evening, Gillian.'

'Sir.'

'The media are going crazy,' continued Curtis. 'God knows how they found out about it.'

'I saw that the circus had turned up outside,' said Harris. 'What have you told them?'

'Just that we've found a body and that it may be John Graydon but we cannot say for certain. When will you be able to confirm identity? It should be fairly straightforward, yes?'

23

'Doc's doing the PM now but as for straightforward...
Look, I suspect you don't want to hear this but I'm not
sure that it's him.'

'Surely it's obvious.'

'Too obvious.'

'But the media are expecting us to confirm that it's
him.'

'As long as you kept it vague, that should give us
enough time to get to the bottom of things,' said Harris.

The commander did not reply.

'You did keep it vague, didn't you?' said Harris. He
gave the superintendent a hard look.

'I may have given them a steer,' said Curtis
uncomfortably. 'I said they were pretty safe to assume that
it's Graydon. Oh, don't look like that, Jack. What else do
you expect me to do? The man's in an aircraft seat with his
number on it, for God's sake. Who else could it be? I
mean, it's hardly going to be Amelia Earhart, is it?'

'Funny how her name keeps cropping up. Perhaps we
should...'

'Until we hear anything different, we assume it's him,'
said Curtis brusquely. He stood up. 'And I do not want us
wasting too much time on it unless we have good reason. I
told the Chief Constable that we would start that anti-
burglary initiative on Friday night, and the last thing I want
is members of your team gallivanting round the hills on a
wild goose chase.'

A bedraggled Matty Gallagher appeared at the office
door, with his hair damp and matted, and his face mud-
stained. Curtis looked him up and down.

'I rest my case,' he said.

Harris looked gloomily at the sergeant.

'Boy, your timing is bad,' he said.

'Sorry,' said Gallagher. 'Anyway, I came to tell you that
Doc's at front counter.'

'What does he want?' asked Curtis. 'He doesn't
normally come here.'

'Says it is important.'

'Must be. He hates stairs. I imagine I'll get another ear-bashing about the lift.' Curtis looked suspiciously at the knowing expression on Harris's face. 'Is this your doing, Jack?'

'Might be,' said Harris. 'Show him up, will you, Matty lad?'

* * *

Five minutes later, the white-haired Home Office pathologist hobbled into the room, sat down heavily and propped his stick against the inspector's desk. After wincing in pain and rubbing his arthritic knee, he noticed them all watching him expectantly.

'When are you going to get that bloody lift installed?' he said grumpily, giving the commander a look. 'Discrimination against the disabled, that's what this is. There's a law against that.'

'You could have phoned,' said Curtis tetchily.

'I wanted to deliver the news in person. This one's a Bobby Dazzler. Hawk, you were right to be suspicious. The body's definitely male but, whoever he is, he's not John Graydon.'

'How on earth can you say?' protested Curtis. 'You've hardly had time to examine it.'

'I don't need much time, Superintendent. Not only is he the wrong age but, as far as I know, John Graydon was not Chinese.'

Even Harris looked surprised.

'Chinese?' he said. 'You sure, Doc?'

'Absolutely. And you're two for two, my boy, because you are also right that he didn't get those injuries falling out of an aeroplane.'

'Will someone tell me what the hell is going on?' said Curtis. He looked in exasperation at Harris. 'If he didn't come from an aeroplane, where on earth did he come from?'

25

'Earth's right,' said the inspector. 'I think that someone is playing games.'

'Some game,' grunted Curtis. He closed his eyes. 'What am I going to tell the media?'

Gillian Roberts' mobile phone rang. She glanced at the read-out.

'It's Alison Butterfield from the hospital,' said the detective inspector. 'Hopefully, she can shed some light on matters.'

She placed the smartphone on the desk with the speaker on.

'Alison,' said Harris, leaning forward slightly. 'Please tell me that you have got them.'

'I am afraid not, sir,' said the detective constable. 'By the time we arrived, they had long gone. Turns out that the girl discharged herself a few minutes after she was asked to wait in A & E.'

'Why the hell did no one tell us?' exclaimed Harris.

'No one noticed.'

'How was that allowed to happen?' said Curtis irritably. He glowered at Harris.

'Good question,' said the inspector. 'Care to enlighten us, Constable?'

'They've been really busy,' replied Butterfield. 'She was not judged to be a serious medical case so it was a while before anyone checked on her. Also, because they did not think it was a police matter, no one told us she had gone. Anyway, there's no sign of her or her boyfriend now.'

'OK, stay there,' said Harris. He looked at Gallagher. 'We're on our way.'

'I'm on my way back down there as well,' said the pathologist. 'And since you'll be at the hospital, gentlemen, there's something you need to see. Those injuries on the skeleton? Not only were they not done falling from a plane, there's no way that they were done twenty years ago either. They're much more recent.'

'Brilliant,' said Curtis and closed his eyes.

Chapter four

It took a grim-faced Jack Harris half an hour to drive to Roxham, the division's largest town, which lay at the bottom of the valley. During the trip along dark and winding country roads, the Land Rover was followed by a saloon car, at the wheel of which was Matty Gallagher, who lived in the town and planned to go home once the night's activities were concluded.

The detectives arrived at the General Hospital shortly after eight and walked into the A & E department, which had begun to empty as cases were dealt with. They were approached by a young short-haired blonde woman in a dark suit and a tall man wearing a green coat.

'They are still missing, I take it?' asked Harris.

'Still missing,' said Alison Butterfield. 'No one has seen them since they walked out of here, and that was more than three hours ago.'

'We've got uniform out looking for them,' said Detective Constable Alistair Marshall. 'Nothing yet, though.'

'They'll be well gone by now,' said Harris. 'The names they were using were fake, I assume?'

'Looks like it,' said Marshall. 'We're still checking but nothing so far that points to their real identities.'

'And the girl's injuries were just play-acting?' said Gallagher.

'What injuries?' said Butterfield. 'Once they got her in here, she said that she felt much better and wanted to go home. The doctors said they were going to do an X-ray just to be sure but by the time they came to take her along, she'd vanished with her boyfriend in tow.'

'What's their game, guv?' asked Marshall. 'And what have they got to do with the body on the hill? Is it definitely John Graydon?'

'No, it's not,' said the inspector. 'As to who he is and what it's about, I am not quite sure yet. I am hoping that the Doc can cast some light on things.'

Harris turned to go.

'Keep searching for them, will you?' he said. 'Bring in more people if you think you need them. I want these two lifted ASAP. We've already wasted enough time on this, as it is.'

Harris and Gallagher left A & E and walked in silence through largely deserted corridors until they reached the mortuary. When they pushed their way through the door, the pathologist was leaning over the skeleton, which had been transferred to a table.

'Hello again, gentlemen,' he said. Doc smiled an apologetic welcome. 'I rather fear that I have made your evening somewhat complicated.'

'You certainly have,' said Harris. 'I'm with Curtis. He was rather hoping that this would be straightforward. There's a ceremony in the parish church to mark the anniversary of the crash at the end of the month and it would be nice to have this all wrapped up before then.'

Matty Gallagher walked over to the table and looked thoughtfully down at the skeleton. Staring into the empty eye sockets, he shuddered as he recalled his time in the wood and the long walk back to the vehicles with darkness falling, the wind lashing rain into his face, and his feet aching from the endless trudge across the moor. The others knew the hills, but Gallagher had felt a long way from the world he understood and had repeatedly stumbled as he tried to follow the route picked out by the inspector's torch beam. Among the many things that Gallagher had struggled with since his move from London, the dark days of winter were the most problematic and he sensed that this afternoon's experience would stay with him for a long time. Staring down at the skeleton, the sergeant wondered if he'd ever feel warm again.

He noticed the others looking at him, expecting him to say something, and wrenched his mind back to the job in hand.

'Back in the office,' he said, looking at the pathologist, 'you mentioned something about the injuries being recent? Not from the time of the air crash?'

'Yes, I did.' Doc leaned over the body and traced his fingers along a couple of fractures on the ribs. 'I would have expected different fracture patterns. No, I think that the injuries were inflicted on terra firma.'

'Any idea when?' asked Harris.

'Last few days maybe, they look fresh. Made with some sort of implement, I would suggest. And not a particularly sharp one either. Something like a baseball bat. If you ask me, someone inflicted a severe beating on our friend here.'

'When he was alive?' asked Harris. 'Are we looking at a murder? Because if we are, that changes everything.'

'I'm not sure.' Doc frowned. 'Not yet anyway. There's still too much about this that does not add up, Hawk. Hopefully, I'll be able to be more definite when I have done a more thorough examination.'

Gallagher looked at the skeleton again.

'So, if it's not John Graydon, who is it?' he asked. He looked at Harris. 'The valley is not exactly overrun with Chinese people. It's hardly a hotbed of multi-culturalism, is it? Julie's Dad voted for Brexit because he saw someone from Carlisle in the Co-Op.'

'It's not quite that bad,' said Harris but he was smiling. 'Any ideas where our Chinese guy came from, Doc?'

'We're trying to get a DNA match.' The pathologist looked down at the body. 'However, for the moment, gentlemen, what you have on your hands is a good old-fashioned John Doe.'

The inspector's mobile rang and he put the device on speaker.

'It's Beth at Forensics,' said a voice. 'You're right about there being a rabbit away. We don't think the seat belongs to an Astra Galaxy, for starters. Also, we don't think that the 'Eleven' is the right label. We think it might have been put on separately. And it looks home-made. I'd say your suspicions are spot on, Jack. Someone went to a lot of trouble to make this look genuine.'

'They certainly did,' said the inspector.

'My money's on students,' said Gallagher as Harris slipped his phone back into his coat pocket. 'Some kind of project, maybe.'

'And the skeleton?' asked Harris. 'How would students get hold of a dead body?'

'Might not be that difficult. Could be one of those that medical students use. I once investigated a break-in at a London teaching hospital and they had a room full of them. A couple of days before Halloween. Spooky, it was. Made the front page of The Standard.'

'It could be a medical one,' said Doc. 'I was coming round to that way of thinking myself.'

The inspector's mobile phone rang again.

'Bloody hell, it never stops,' he said wearily.

'It's Gillian,' said the detective inspector when Harris took the call. 'You had best take a look on YouTube. Key in *The Death of Passenger Eleven.*'

A couple of minutes later, Harris, Gallagher and the Doc were crowded round the sergeant's smartphone, watching in growing amazement as the film unfolded on the screen. Beginning with dramatic music for the titles, but giving no names for the film-makers, it showed archive footage of the Astra Galaxy wreckage strewn across the northern hills before switching to images of Harris and Mike Ganton taken in the wood that afternoon. The commentary, delivered by a young man's voice in stentorian tones, was accompanied by footage taken behind the two rescuers as they picked their way precariously down the slope, occasionally grabbing hold of tree trunks to steady themselves.

'Little bastard,' murmured Harris.

Finally, the film showed grainy footage of the two men finding the skeleton and moving in closer to examine the body, the shock etched clearly on their faces.

'But is it really John Graydon?' intoned the commentator. 'Did the fraudster take the ultimate fall for his crimes, after all? Did he really pay the ultimate price? And whose money did he use? It's over to DCI Jack Harris and his team of dedicated boys and girls to find out. Watch this space!'

'Definitely students,' said Gallagher when the closing music had faded away. 'It's got that kind of look about it.'

'I think you're probably right,' said Harris. He looked at the pathologist. 'Best get our John Doe processed quickly, Doc.'

'Why?'

'Because,' said a scowling inspector, heading for the door, 'when I find the little toerag that shot that footage, I'm going to ring his fucking neck. That's why.'

'And folks say that he has no sense of humour,' said Gallagher brightly.

Chapter five

Shortly after 8am the next morning, Jack Harris gathered a small team of officers in the CID room at Levton Bridge Police Station. Pinned to the board behind where he was standing was a blown-up image taken from the YouTube video, showing the skeleton sitting on the wooded slope and grinning out at the officers, as if mocking them. The atmosphere among the detectives was light-hearted; the realisation that they were probably dealing with nothing more sinister than a student prank had infused the inquiry with a sense of levity.

Seated in the front row, Matty Gallagher was regaling colleagues with his escapades of the previous afternoon and several of them were smiling as he gesticulated wildly to illustrate one of his jokes.

Jack Harris was not smiling.

'Thank you,' he said.

The conversations did not die down.

'Thank you,' he said, louder this time.

Silence settled on the room as the officers watched the inspector turn to tap the image on the board then look sternly back to his detectives.

'I appreciate that this could be viewed as somewhat amusing,' he said, 'but do not make the mistake of writing it off as a joke. This is a deadly serious matter and I want it to be treated as such.'

'But it's just a bunch of students,' protested Alistair Marshall, who was sitting in the front row. The detective constable looked round at the others for support. 'I did the same kind of thing when I was at uni. Not this elaborate, I grant you, but just as daft. Haven't we got more important things to do than chase a bunch of kids?'

'But that's the point, is it not?' Harris's voice hardened as he stared at the young constable. 'Might I remind you, Alistair, that not only have these people wasted a lot of our time but they have tried to make us look stupid in the process. And I, for one, do not like people making me out to be stupid. It might also be worth remembering that they have made light of one of the most traumatic events in this valley's history. Fourteen people died in that crash. Fourteen, ladies and gentlemen. Eight kids lost parents that night. We should never forget that.'

With the inspector's tone suggesting that he would brook no dissent, smiles vanished from faces and a more sombre atmosphere settled on the room. Alistair Marshall nodded meekly and stared at his shoes, resolving to stay quiet in the face of the inspector's irritation; everyone knew from hard experience that you did not cross an irritated Jack Harris.

'What's more,' continued Harris, 'even though the press office has issued a statement making clear that this is a hoax, there will still be some people who think that we really have found John Graydon. I, for one, have had enough of the conspiracy theories so I want these jokers brought to book.'

'What will we charge them with when we find them?' asked Alison Butterfield, who was sitting next to Alistair Marshall. 'Wasting police time, I am guessing?'

'And anything else that we can get to stick,' said Harris. 'Making a malicious emergency call, for one. The mountain rescue guys are livid that they were called out to risk their lives in such bad conditions because someone thought it would be funny. The chopper crew feel the same. By rights, they shouldn't really have made that last flight. What if they'd crashed? Wouldn't be funny then, would it?'

Several officers shook their heads; the inspector's tight-lipped anger was making a big impact on them. Alistair Marshall looked as respectful as he could and tried not to catch his boss's eye.

'What's more,' said Harris, 'someone inflicted the injuries on our John Doe. This could still turn out to be a murder inquiry. What do we have so far, Matty lad?'

'We are working on the basis that the film-makers could be media students,' said Gallagher. 'Our Geek Squad say that the film is quite well put together so we are wondering if it may be some kind of coursework. A college maybe. Or a university.'

The sergeant held up a computer print-out.

'This is a list of places in the North that run courses like that,' he said.

'Let's get onto them then,' said Harris. 'See if we can find anyone with links to this area. The body was found well away from the main walking trails so it's a reasonable assumption that we're looking for someone with a bit of local knowledge.'

'Hang on,' said Butterfield. She looked at Marshall. 'I'd forgotten. Didn't Davie Tinkler go off to do media studies last year?'

'I think you may be right,' said Marshall. 'His mum mentioned it when we saw her at that Neighbourhood Watch meeting, didn't she? He's at Newcastle Uni, I think.'

'Well, they're definitely on the list,' said Gallagher. He ran his finger down his piece of paper. 'Yeah, here we are, Film and Media BA Honours, whatever the hell that is.'

'Yes, but it wasn't him on the hill yesterday afternoon, was it?' said Harris. 'I didn't recognise either the lad or his supposed girlfriend.'

'But it did not need to be him, did it?' said the sergeant. 'All he had to do was get someone else to stage the accident. Someone he knew would not be recognised.'

'Yeah,' said Butterfield. 'And, now I think about it, his dad is a sheep farmer over that way so Davie probably knows the area better than most people.'

Harris turned back to the board and looked at the image of the grinning skull.

'Would he be up to something like this, though?' he asked. The inspector turned back to Butterfield. 'Davie Tinkler always struck me as a bit dozy. Like it or not, this is pretty imaginative stuff.'

'Yes, but he has always been a bit of a creative character,' said Butterfield. 'Bit arty. He's pretty young for his age and very naïve, too – maybe he did not realise how much trouble he was causing.'

'Well, he's as good a place as any to begin,' said Harris. 'Ring his parents, will you, Alison? See if they know what he's been up to – and find out if he's been home recently. Gillian, any leads on the identity of our John Doe?'

'Nothing definite,' said the detective inspector. 'But the idea that it's a medical specimen for students does seem to be our best option. We are going to check the medical schools.'

'Well, start with Newcastle,' said Gallagher. 'It's got a big one. Bit of a coincidence in the circumstances.'

'OK, folks,' said Harris. He clapped his hands. 'It sounds like we may be getting somewhere. We're supposed to be launching the Super's anti-burglary initiative on Friday night and he keeps bending my ear about it, so I want this thing wrapped up before then. Today, if we can.'

* * *

Twenty minutes later, the inspector was sitting in his office, sipping his mug of tea and catching up on paperwork, when Gallagher walked in with a broad smile on his face.

'I sense that you have news,' said the inspector.

'Sure do. All but solved this one on the blower.'

'Curtis will be pleased.' Harris held up a memo. 'He's been banging on about mileage again. How did you do it?'

I got hold of one of Davie Tinkler's lecturers and he reckons that a group of them *were* working on a film. The lecturers were giving them technical advice but the kids wouldn't tell them what it was about.'

'Did Alison get through to Davie's parents?'

'Yeah. Mum was a bit vague on what he actually does at uni but she did confirm that Davie was home at the weekend. What's more, the shepherd who saw the plane go down? Turns out he was Davie's uncle, so the kid grew up with stories of the incident. It had always fascinated him, apparently. Oh, and guess who was with Davie on his weekend visit home?'

'His girlfriend?'

'The very same. Care to guess what she's studying?'

'Not medicine at Newcastle University, by any chance?'

'Funny that, isn't it?' said Gallagher. 'I reckon we can wrap this up pretty quickly, guv, just like you wanted. Looks like Mister Curtis will get his anti-burglary initiative, after all.'

'OK, get over there,' said Harris. 'Take Alison. She knows Davie. If you have to lean on him and his pals, you've got my backing. Put the fear of God into them, yeah?'

'How about I put the fear of Jack Harris into them instead?'

'I always thought that it was the same thing anyway.'

'Excellent,' replied Gallagher approvingly. 'Your sense of humour is coming on nicely. A bit more work and my job here will soon be done and I can return to my own planet.'

'Get out,' said Harris.

* * *

Gallagher was still chuckling as he and Butterfield walked across the yard and got into the sergeant's car. Shortly before noon, the detectives were walking down a fourth-floor corridor in one of the Newcastle University buildings when the sergeant recognised a bespectacled young man who had just emerged from a classroom in front of them, a battered rucksack slung over his shoulder.

'Don't tell me,' said the sergeant in a loud voice. 'You'd always fancied a nice ride in a shiny yellow helicopter?'

The student turned and the colour drained from his face as he stared in horror at the approaching detectives.

'How's the girlfriend?' said Gallagher; he was enjoying himself. 'Recovered from her headache, has she? Remarkable what you can do with a couple of paracetamol. Walked out of the hospital unaided, I'm told.'

'Bollocks,' said the student.

'Very eloquent,' replied Gallagher. He winked at Butterfield. 'Amazing what a university education can do for you, is it not, Constable?'

'Oh, aye.'

A young man dressed in scruffy jeans and a faded blue T-shirt, with long and lank unwashed black hair, emerged from the room, saw the detectives and turned quickly away.

'Davie Tinkler?' said Gallagher. He glanced at Butterfield, who nodded.

Tinkler gave the officers a sullen look.

'Yeah, what of it?' he asked.

'DS Gallagher from Levton Bridge.' Gallagher flashed his warrant card. 'I think you know DC Butterfield. We want to talk to you about a film that went up on YouTube last night.'

'I know nowt about it.' Tinkler turned to walk away. 'Now, we've got another lecture to go to so if you…'

'Here's a little thought to consider before you go,' said the sergeant. His affability had been replaced by a harder edge. 'As it stands, you've only got me and the constable here to worry about and we're fairly easy-going types. However, muck us about and we may have to ask our governor to come over.'

Tinkler looked worried.

'Your governor?' he asked uneasily.

'Yeah, DCI Harris, now he's really pissed off with you.' Gallagher shook his head. 'I mean, *really* pissed off, eh, Constable?'

'Sure is,' said Butterfield. She, too, was enjoying the impact that the sergeant's words were having on the anxious students. 'I'm not sure that I have ever seen him so angry. Says that he does not like folks trying to make him look stupid.'

'Come on, Tinks,' said the other student. 'The game's up.'

Davie Tinkler gave the detectives a glum look.

'What do you want to know?' he asked with a sigh.

The detective gestured for the students to go back into the room. Once Gallagher had closed the door, he wandered over to the window and looked down on to a scene bustling with life. As he watched students walking across the quadrangle and the vehicles heading along the nearby road, and heard the sound of voices and the hoot of car horns, Gallagher sighed; God, how he had missed such sights and sounds since his move to the valley.

Recalling the reason for his presence in Newcastle, Gallagher turned back to the students, who had sat down at one of the desks and were staring at him, their unease growing at the lengthening silence.

'What I want to know,' said Gallagher, without moving away from the window, 'is do you have any idea what harm you have caused?'

'What harm?' protested Tinkler. 'It was just a bit of fun.'

'DCI Harris would venture to disagree,' said the sergeant. He turned back into the room. 'I know that because I had to sit through one of his lectures on the subject this morning. Less enjoyable than yours, I would imagine. For a start, do you know how much it costs to launch a RAF rescue helicopter?'

The students shook their heads.

'Thousands,' said Gallagher. 'At this rate, you'll still be paying off your student loans when you're ninety.'

'You can't make us pay for that!' exclaimed Tinkler.

'Can't I?' Gallagher gave him a stern look. 'There is such an offence as making a malicious emergency call, you know?'

'Malicious!' exclaimed the other student. 'We weren't being malicious!' We meant no one no harm. Like Tinks says, it was just a bit of fun!'

'I'm not sure you quite realise how much trouble you are in,' said the sergeant, intensifying his stare. 'All those people putting themselves at risk for some stupid kids who thought they were having a bit of fun.'

'Yes, but…'

'And I'm pretty sure that the university will want to consider whether or not to kick you off your course when they find out what has been happening.'

'But we did it for one of their modules,' protested Tinkler.

'Maybe you did, son, but I can't see your Vice-Chancellor being impressed when the university's name is dragged through the mud, can you?' The sergeant recalled the long walk on the hill the previous afternoon and thought of his caked boots sitting back in the squad room. 'And I, for one, have had enough of being dragged through the mud.'

Chapter six

It was shortly after noon when Detective Inspector Jenny Armannsson, the newly-appointed head of Greater Manchester Police's Fraud Squad, settled down with a cup of coffee at the desk in her austere third-floor city centre office. She gave a heavy sigh as she started to leaf through the reports that had piled up in her in-tray while she and her team focused on the rumour that John Graydon was still alive. Not that all the reports dated from when she had taken on the job; her predecessor had let them pile up as well – deliberately, in Armannsson's view. More focused on his retirement than solving crime, he had offered little support in their handover meeting and had made little secret of his belief that she was not the right person to take over from him.

For her part, Armannsson had not believed the tip-off from the anonymous informant that had prompted renewed interest in the Graydon case. His call to the office to claim that John Graydon was living in the Cayman Islands was just another in a series over the years putting him everywhere from Bolivia to Thailand; and Armannsson knew what a wild goose chase looked like. However, her orders from the Chief Constable were simple; 'I want this sorted, Jenny,' he had said sternly. 'If he's alive, I want him locked up. And the others, I want them as well'.

As a new head of department just days into her role, Armannsson had not felt confident enough to challenge him. She could have done without the task, though – she was acutely aware that her predecessor was not the only one who doubted her abilities. She knew what older male colleagues were saying about her. Too young to run a department like Fraud. A woman. Blonde. Armannsson knew that they would seize on her failure to track down Graydon and his acolytes as proof of her inadequacy. Her mood was little improved when the chief rang her at home first thing that morning to make it clear that the hoax about the skeleton changed nothing. This was still a live investigation, he had said.

She looked up with relief when her reading was disturbed by one of her team, who gave a heavy knock on the door and walked into the room. She tried not to look disappointed when she saw that it was Danny Caulker.

'Have you checked the Graydon accounts yet?' she asked.

'Sure have.' He held up a series of computer print-outs. 'And interesting reading they make.'

His voice hinted at barely-supressed excitement. Armannsson was intrigued. It was the first time she had seen the detective constable enthusiastic since her appointment; he had tended to treat her with a surly indifference bordering on hostility.

'Why?' she asked.

'The words "cat" and "pigeons" spring readily to mind, I would suggest.'

Caulker, a veteran officer who had spent eight years with the squad, placed the pieces of paper on the desk and slid them across towards her. He watched with faint amusement as Armannsson's eyes widened as she leafed through the pages one by one, then flicked back again to ensure that she had interpreted the rows of numbers correctly.

'Yeah, you read it right,' he said.

'Is this for real?' The detective inspector looked up at him with astonishment etched on her face. 'Are we sure it's genuine?'

'As sure as we can be,' said Caulker. 'It happened last night. Graydon's money is on the move, alright.'

Armannsson looked back at the pieces of paper and shook her head.

'Twenty years, Danny,' she said. 'Twenty years without so much as a dicky bird and now this. It's going to make Jack Harris's life considerably more complicated, I can tell you. He is not going to be happy about it.'

'Jack Harris is never happy.'

'No, indeed,' said Armannsson. She pushed the print-outs back across the table. 'Which is why I want us to double check this. I don't want us looking stupid. From what I have heard of Harris, he is not the type to suffer fools gladly. We need to make sure that no one is playing silly buggers.'

'But how could they be, ma'am? No one knows that we have been monitoring the bank accounts.'

'I appreciate that, Danny, but let's make sure, anyway. I mean, it's one hell of a coincidence that this should happen just hours after the skeleton was found, isn't it?'

'Maybe not,' said Caulker. 'What if it's entirely to be expected?'

'Go on.'

Caulker sat down at the desk.

'Let's assume that the rumours are right,' he said, 'and that John Graydon really is still alive. What if he hears about the skeleton before it's revealed to be a hoax? It's been getting international coverage and it would not take long for him to hear about it – even if he is in the Cayman Islands.'

'OK, I'll buy that.'

'So, if he thought it was a genuine discovery, it's also reasonable to assume that he realised that it wouldn't be long before we worked out that whoever Passenger Eleven was, it wasn't him. So, what does he do?'

'He panics.'

'He panics.' Caulker tapped the print-outs. 'And moves the money. Who knows, we may get that jolly holi' to the Cayman Islands, after all.'

The constable gave his boss a sly look.

'You'd look good in a swimsuit,' he said.

Armannsson sighed.

'And you were doing so well,' she said.

There was silence in the room for a few moments as Armannsson debated whether or not to tell Caulker exactly what she thought of him and he spent the time wondering if he had overstepped the mark with the comment. In the end, she decided to keep it professional.

'I guess all of this does back up what our anonymous caller has been telling us,' she said. 'Time to tell Jack Harris about his other claim as well, I think.'

'Is that wise? I thought that the chief wanted GMP to handle it?'

'He does, but he says that we have to give them first crack at it. Protocol, Danny. I've just been trying to figure out the best way to phrase it.'

'Is the chief really sure that they can handle something that big? It's a woolly-back force, remember.'

'Maybe so, Danny, but the plane did come down in their area. Maybe they'll be only too pleased to hand it back to us.'

'You don't know Jack Harris,' said Caulker. 'He'll jump at something like this.'

'Then I imagine it'll get very political. Who knows, it may end up in a joint investigation?' Her time to give the sly look. 'Hey, you might be able to reacquaint yourself with your old pal. I hear you're big buddies.'

Danny Caulker thought of the last time he had met Harris and looked less than enthusiastic at the prospect of meeting him again.

'Looking forward to it already,' he said.

'I bet you are.'

Chapter seven

'So, they admitted making the film then?' said Harris. He tipped back in his chair and looked at Gallagher with undisguised satisfaction. 'Just like that?'

'Yeah, they admitted it alright.' Gallagher sat down at the desk. 'I thought for a moment that young Davie was going to brazen it out but, for some reason, that changed when we told him that you were hacked off with him. You two got previous?'

'I may have cuffed him around the ear once or twice. Had he not thought it through?'

'Do students ever think things through?'

'I guess not,' said Harris. 'What's the story then?'

'Pretty much as we thought. Davie knew that the twentieth anniversary of the air crash was coming up and roped in two students on his course, including the lad who pretended to be the boyfriend.' Gallagher passed a hand dramatically across his brow. 'He was all for it, apparently, da-aaarling. He wants to be an *actor*, don't you know? His mother played a barmaid in Hollyoaks.'

Harris looked nonplussed.

'Sorry,' said Gallagher. 'I keep forgetting that you don't do cultural references.'

'And the aeroplane seat?' Harris had ignored the sergeant's comment. 'Where did they get hold of that?'

'eBay. We checked, it's dead easy to get hold of them. And not that expensive either. I'm thinking of getting one for the lounge if Julie agrees. There's a nice one in mauve. They made the number tag themselves in one of the university's workshops.'

'And the body?' asked Harris. 'Where did that come from?'

'Ah, well that's where it gets a bit more murky. The girl got it through some lad she knows at a local hospital. She refused to tell us who he was but I don't think it'll take much work to track him down. From what she said, he's not a medical person so our money's on a porter or someone like that.'

'And, pray, where did a humble porter get hold of a skeleton?'

'We may have an idea about that as well,' said the sergeant. 'I rang a mate of mine in the National Crime Agency to see if he knew. Turns out a number of them have been in circulation over recent months and they're trying to find out why. They're sending someone up to talk to the kids.'

'What about the injuries to our John Doe?'

'Inflicted post-mortem, like Doc thought. The students thumped it with a croquet mallet, of all things.'

'Sounds like it's all come together nicely.' Harris tipped his chair forward and reached for his tea. 'So where did you leave things?'

'I told the students that we'd talk to the CPS. Didn't tell them about the National Crime Agency. I left that as a little surprise. They were terrified enough by the time we'd finished with them. Something like this does not look good on a CV.'

'I'm sure it doesn't.' Harris gave a nod of satisfaction and downed the last of his drink. 'Excellent work, Matty lad. Excellent work.'

'It was Alison who first mentioned Davie Tinkler. She deserves a lot of the credit.'

'Yeah, I'll have a word with her.' Harris gave a rare smile. 'Curtis will be happy.'

'About what?' asked the commander as he walked into the office. He glanced at the inspector's dogs curled up by the radiator but made no comment.

'We have wrapped up the film inquiry,' said Harris. 'Like you wanted, all very straightforward. Might even get that fishing trip in with Leckie.'

'Only once you have launched the burglary initiative,' said Curtis quickly. 'I am sure you have not forgotten about that.'

'How could I, sir?'

The inspector's desk phone rang. He took the call.

'Is that Jack Harris?' said a woman's voice.

'Speaking.'

'This is Detective Inspector Jenny Armannsson from the Greater Manchester Fraud Squad. Graham Leckie suggested I ring you.'

'Yeah, he mentioned you. I was going to ring when I got the chance. You've probably heard that the body is a hoax by now, yes? Wherever John Graydon is, he's certainly not lying in our mortuary. It's all very straightforward at this end.'

'I wouldn't be so sure about that,' said Armannsson. 'See, something strange happened after the story broke that Graydon's body had been found. To do with a number of offshore bank accounts set up in assumed names just before he disappeared.'

'Not sure I like the way this is going.' Harris glanced at Curtis. The commander had begun to look worried. 'Certainly does not sound that straightforward.'

'That's the last word I would use,' said Armannsson. 'See, we have been monitoring the accounts for twenty years. From the early days of the original investigation, in fact. We are pretty sure Graydon thought we did not know about them. We only check now and then because nothing ever happens. The bank wanted to close them down at one stage because they only contained peanuts, but my predecessor persuaded them to keep them open – just in case. About the only good thing he ever did. Anyway, once news broke about the body, we did a quick check and a series of payments were made into them last night.'

'Really?' said Harris in a hollow voice. The ramifications of her words were already playing out in his mind and none of them were good. 'How much are we talking about, Jenny?'

'Twelve million quid, give or take.'

Harris gave a low whistle.

'So much for peanuts,' he said.

'Exactly,' said Armannsson. 'The money was not in them for long – it was moved on within minutes, but the accounts were definitely in use.'

'Which means?'

'You know exactly what it means,' said Armannsson. 'And there's something else you need to know. We've got an informant who says that the plane was sabotaged.'

'And do you believe him?'

Armannsson thought of her Chief Constable's eager desire to see John Graydon brought to justice.

'I think I have to,' she said.

After finishing the call, the inspector looked at the others; it seemed to them that his cheeks had lost some of their usual colour.

'What's the problem, Jack?' asked Curtis. 'You look like you've seen a ghost.'

'Perhaps I have,' said Harris.

* * *

After concluding the call to Harris, Jenny Armannsson glanced up at the wall clock in her office and realised that she was late for her meeting with the chief constable. Cursing, she stood up, switched off her laptop and had just taken her coat down from the hook when one of the phones rang in the deserted squad room. She sighed, walked over to the desk and picked up the receiver. There was silence for a few moments but she could hear breathing on the other end.

'Hello,' said Armannsson. 'Who is this?'

More silence, more breathing.

'Look, I know you are there,' she said. 'If you're going to ask what colour my knickers are, will you get on with it? I'm late for an app…'

'Are you going to re-open the inquiry?' said a man's muffled voice.

'What inquiry?'

'You know what inquiry,' said the man. 'Into the crash?'

'I don't know what we are going to do yet,' said the inspector. 'Is there anything else you can tell us which might…?'

But the line went dead.

* * *

'There's no way we can handle this,' said Philip Curtis. He looked across his desk at Harris. 'Not on our own, not with our limited resources. The chief agrees.'

'Yes, well, I'm not giving it away,' said Harris. Defiance flashed in his eyes. 'You don't get the chance to go after something like this very often in a career.'

Their body language told its own story; it was early evening and, following a flurry of activity, the two men had been discussing the matter for thirty minutes, the conversation going in circles, becoming ever more fractious as it did so.

'This isn't about personal glory, Jack,' said Curtis.

'It never is,' snapped the inspector. 'And you don't know me very well if you think that I look at things that way.'

'Sorry,' said Curtis quickly, seeking to defuse the situation. 'That was uncalled for. And I do know you better than that.'

'I just think that this should be our inquiry. That plane came down in our patch and, because Air Accident ran the inquiry last time, this force was never afforded the opportunity to mount a criminal investigation.'

'Yes, but that was because no one suspected that it was anything other than a tragic accident.'

'I appreciate that, sir,' said Harris. He sensed that a more respectful approach was called for. 'And I am not blaming anyone for the decisions that were taken, but the suggestion that the plane was brought down changes everything.'

'Yes, but do we believe it? It's all pretty tenuous. We could end up wasting a lot of time, not to mention money. And end up looking pretty stupid if it's some crank.'

'Think what would happen if it got out that we ignored it, though.'

There was silence for a few moments as the men eyed each other unhappily. In the early days of the commander's tenure at Levton Bridge, most of their meetings had been like this, but now that they had found a way of working together, neither man was relishing such a profound disagreement.

'If you don't think I'm up to it, just say so,' said Harris. 'If that's what this is really about...'

'Of course, it's not,' said Curtis. 'I am fully aware that you made your name handling extremely complex cases when you were in Manchester, but you are just one man. And quite a few of your team are very young.'

'Then we bring in officers from other divisions. Jenny Armannsson and her team can handle the fraud side of it, if that's what is worrying the chief.'

Curtis hesitated.

'There's something else, isn't there?' said Harris.

'He has already decided to hand the whole case over to Manchester. Their Chief Constable has been pushing hard for it. Says that it's way beyond our capabilities.'

'He's just saying that to wind me up!' exclaimed Harris angrily. 'The man has never liked me.'

Curtis looked at the detective chief inspector; did he detect a sense of hurt? If he did, it was the first time that the detective had allowed himself to show his vulnerable side to his commander. The room fell silent again.

'Have you ever met him?' asked Harris eventually. 'Their chief?'

Memories stirred within Curtis of the only time he had encountered the man. It had been seven years previously at a superintendent's conference and he could still hear the laughter when his Manchester counterpart had referred to the force as a 'rural backwater full of sheep'. The commander recalled his embarrassment as his cheeks had reddened.

'Yes, I have,' said the commander. 'Let me have another word.'

Chapter eight

The atmosphere in the briefing room the next morning was in stark contrast to the levity of twenty-four hours previously. Jack Harris stood at the front of the room and surveyed with grim satisfaction the ranks of uniformed and plainclothes men and women. More than thirty officers had arrived at Levton Bridge Police Station in a state of high anticipation, each one of them eager to hear what the inspector was about to say. Rumours sweeping the station had suggested that he would be making an announcement about the air crash, speculation now confirmed by the image pinned to the noticeboard behind him, a large photograph depicting wreckage from the Astra Galaxy strewn across a hillside, some of it obscured by wisps of drifting smoke.

Everyone in the room found their gaze continually drawn to the image; for many, it brought back memories of one of the darkest episodes in the valley's history. A number of them had been on duty that night and, sitting in the briefing room, they were transported back twenty years to burning aviation fuel that stung sharp and acrid at the back of the throat, to the sickening stench of scorched flesh that turned the stomach and to the constant clatter of rotor blades as rescue helicopters hovered perilously low over the windswept hillside in the increasingly desperate search for survivors.

One more image came to many of the officers' minds, a horror that had only been revealed when the pale glimmer of dawn cast its watery light across the hills, washing them in shades of horror. Bodies. All the bodies. Sitting there now, those officers remembered the footage filmed by a television station helicopter, which showed lines of orange-clad mountain rescue teams picking their way slowly down the hillside as they carried the shrouded dead the four miles to a fleet of waiting ambulances.

Watching the officers' reaction, Harris could not conceal the slightest of smiles. Although he had returned to the valley in search of peace, the inspector still relished the opportunity to be at the heart of something big from time to time, a throwback to his former life. Having left the valley to enlist in the army as a teenager, he had always enjoyed the thrill of his involvement in major peacekeeping operations around the world. On leaving the military, he had sought similar excitement with Greater Manchester Police, where he had rapidly risen to the rank of Detective Inspector on the back of a reputation earned by his ability to co-ordinate complex investigations into gangland activities, to target those who others viewed as untouchable.

Surveying the assembled officers, he felt that same excitement now. The expectation in the room was heightened by the presence of three newcomers sitting in the front row: a slim woman in her thirties with short blonde hair and wearing a dark suit; a jowly man with thinning, greying hair, bags beneath his eyes and dressed in an ill-fitting grey suit; and a lean, tall, dark-haired uniformed officer who some of the Levton Bridge officers recognised as Graham Leckie from his previous visits to the area to see his old friend Harris, usually clutching his fishing tackle.

'Ladies and gentlemen,' began Harris. The murmured conversations stopped and the room fell silent. 'Thank you for your attendance, particularly those brought in at short notice from other divisions. Can I also welcome the officers from GMP. DI Jenny Armannsson and DC Danny Caulker are from the Fraud Squad, and many of you know Graham Leckie. I am sure you will afford them all a warm welcome.'

There was a murmur of agreement. One or two of the older Levton Bridge officers shot knowing looks in the direction of Armannsson – everyone had heard the rumours that Jack Harris had, on occasion, afforded the warmest welcomes possible to visiting female officers, particularly attractive blonde ones. Armannsson and her colleagues, for their part, inclined their heads in acknowledgment. The detective inspector had a knowing smile on her face as she watched Harris continue his address; she'd heard the rumours, too. Leckie had made sure of that. 'There's something you need to know about Jack Harris,' he had said conspiratorially as he drew her aside in a corridor before they had left Manchester early that morning.

'You will be aware,' continued Harris, 'that we have experienced a hoax by a bunch of university students trying to convince the world that Passenger Eleven has been found. It would appear that not everyone realised it was a hoax. The news seems to have flushed out the real Mr Graydon.'

More murmurs rippled round the room.

'It would seem,' said Harris, enjoying the reaction, 'that he tried to get at his money. Or someone did, anyway, and, for the moment, because we are working on the premise that it's John Graydon, we will be running a joint investigation with Greater Manchester Police. Our main responsibility at Levton Bridge will be to re-investigate the plane crash.'

'But surely the air investigators put it down to pilot error?' said a plainclothes officer sitting at the back of the room. 'They ignored the dodgy altimeter and slammed into Hobb's Point.'

'That's what the report said, yes. However, there is reason to believe that the crash may have been caused deliberately.'

Excited voices filled the room.

'Settle down,' said Harris. 'This may well have turned into a murder inquiry, ladies and gentlemen, and our job is to find out if the investigators missed anything.'

'You're not going to have us searching the hills for wreckage, are you, Jack?' said another officer. He glanced gloomily at the rain, which was now driving hard and horizontal against the window. 'I haven't got me 'at.'

'And I got altitude sickness yesterday,' said Gallagher, who was sitting in a middle row.

'No,' said the DCI, with a slight smile. He glanced at Philip Curtis, who was leaning against a wall. 'I don't think that will be necessary at this stage. We'll ask mountain rescue if they can spare anyone instead. Oh, and before anyone says it, yes, I know that investigating air crashes is not exactly our thing, so we will be bringing in some expert help. As regards the fraud side of things, I'll let DI Armannsson talk about what her team will be doing.'

Harris stepped back and the detective inspector walked to the front of the room.

'Thank you, Jack,' she said.

Although all eyes had turned to her, the inspector's voice was assured. Confident; excited even. Despite her doubts surrounding the case, Jenny Armannsson knew a career opportunity when she saw one. She also sensed, standing at the front of the room, that she could detect scepticism from some of those present, some who still did not see women as senior officers, others who habitually doubted the ability of largely desk-bound investigators. She relished the opportunity to prove them wrong on both counts and gave a slight smile.

'In case you don't know, we're the lot that don't need hats,' she said. 'We keep nice and dry, thank you very much. And we have plenty of tea and cake.'

The remark did the job and laughter ran round the room. Even Danny Caulker smiled and Harris nodded his approval. Armannsson waited for the laughter to die away.

'We have two tasks,' she said eventually. Her tone was serious. 'Firstly, we have to find out who has been moving John Graydon's cash. We will lead on that part of the inquiry, although we may need to draft in some help from your team, Jack.'

'As long as it's not me,' said Gallagher. 'I struggle to turn my calculator on.'

'Until he comes to add up his expenses,' said a voice. 'Then he finds the right button alright.'

More laughter.

'Our other task,' said Armannsson, smiling at the banter which was something that had been lacking in the fraud squad office since she had taken over, 'is to find John Graydon. And, if we do find him, it'll be down to all of us to discover who on earth Passenger Eleven was.'

She went back to her chair and Harris took centre stage again. He waited for the conversations to fade and for silence to settle on the room.

'One more thing,' he said. 'This looks like it is going to be the biggest inquiry that this force has ever undertaken and there are those who think that it is beyond us.'

The inspector glanced at Danny Caulker, who looked away.

'So, I want this done properly,' continued Harris. 'No cutting corners. Your section leaders will brief you on the next steps.'

With a scraping of chair legs and loud cacophony of voices, the meeting broke up.

The team of officers from the National Crime Agency arrived in Newcastle shortly after nine thirty. Three of them walked into the university's media unit and led a shocked Davie Tinkler and his fellow film-makers out to a waiting car while two more headed for the medical school where they broke into a lecture and led his tearful girlfriend away.

Chapter nine

'The legendary Jack Harris,' said Jenny Armannsson as she walked into the inspector's office thirty minutes after the briefing had finished. She gestured to the chair at the desk. 'May I?'

'Be my guest.' Harris made a perfunctory attempt to tidy up the papers that were always sprawled across his desk. 'Nicely handled back there, by the way. Some of them can be cynical old buggers.'

'Including you, I would imagine.' She sat down. 'Thank you, anyway. Good to work with you.'

'Nice of you to say so. I'm not sure about the legendary bit, though.'

'Your reputation does rather tend to precede you,' said Armannsson.

'I wouldn't believe everything an old sweat like Danny Caulker tells you. He and I were hardly on the best of terms when we worked together.'

'So I gather. Two men with a penchant for doing things their own way, I would venture to suggest.'

'Something like that,' said Harris. He was intrigued by her confidence in addressing a senior officer in such a way; it was the thing that had struck him most in their short meeting in the briefing room before the others arrived. 'What did he say about me then?'

'That you like dogs, whisky and women. In that order.'

'I'd like to think there's a bit more to me than that.'

'I'm sure there is,' said Armannsson. 'When I had just made CID in Stockport, all anyone could talk about was what you and your team were doing with the gangs in Manchester. A lot of the crims were glad when you left.'

'Nice to know that people noticed. I don't remember you, though, Jenny. We did not meet?'

'No, we didn't.'

'I think I'd have remembered,' said Harris.

'I'm sure you would.'

Harris's sense of intrigue increased. For her part, Jenny Armannsson appeared to be amused by the exchange. Leckie had prepared her well for the encounter: be confident and play his game, the constable had said in the car on the way up. Sitting in the back seat, Caulker had given a scornful grunt but said nothing.

'So,' said Harris. 'Since you seem to know everything about me, how about you tell me something about yourself? How come you ended up at GMP? Your surname suggests that you are not exactly local.'

'Actually I am. Salford born and bred. As for the name, it's Icelandic. Anglicised. My father was a police officer in Reykjavík before he met Mum. She was a travel rep from Stockport and they moved there after they got married. Dad got a job in home security.'

'I am not sure I'd have given up Iceland for Stockport,' said Harris.

'Young love.'

'Even so,' said Harris wistfully. 'Iceland is a terrific place, you know. Especially the birds. And before you say anything, it's not what you think. Me and Leckie have always had a thing for wildlife and we went there a few years back to see the great skuas. Remarkable animals are great skuas. Savage as hell but remarkable.'

'Not my bag really.'

'And what is your bag, Detective Inspector?' asked Harris. He eyed her keenly. 'What gets you out of bed in the morning?'

'Catching villains.'

'So, tell me then, Detective Inspector Armannsson.' Harris sat back in his seat and placed his arms behind his head. 'Is John Graydon still alive or are we chasing shadows?'

'I have not made my mind up yet. What do you think?'

'Same. He's either buried in the peat somewhere up on the hills or, and I hate to say this, I really do, or the conspiracy theorists were right all along and he was never on the plane in the first place.'

'Either way, it's always nagged away at our Chief Constable,' said Armannsson. 'That's why we've re-opened the inquiry. He spent some time in the Fraud Squad earlier in his career and he does not think that the original investigation was thorough enough.'

'But Leckie reckons that you've got thirty-five boxes of evidence cluttering up the place. Sounds thorough to me.'

'Most of it's useless. Anyway, when the chief promoted me, he asked me to review the case. I thought that we were wasting our time but we started asking a few questions. Showing willing really. Doesn't do to doubt the wisdom of a Chief Constable.'

'Not a view I've ever taken,' said Harris.

'So I hear.'

'You hear a lot, Detective Inspector. Tell me, where does your anonymous informant fit into the picture?'

'It was odd really. We were not getting anywhere then, a few days ago, he rang the office and said that if we wanted John Graydon, we should look in the Cayman Islands.'

'And did you?'

'As best we could but, surprise, surprise, the chief did not fancy forking out for us to go on a nice holiday and we could not find any evidence that Graydon was there anyway. The Cayman Island authorities were not particularly helpful. Our guy has been on a couple more times but he rings off when we start pushing him.'

'Any idea who he is?'

Armannsson shook her head.

'Nope,' she said. 'But it's one hell of a coincidence that he should get in touch after we started asking questions for the first time in twenty years. He's careful, mind. Difficult to say how old he is as he disguises his voice and he always uses an untraceable number. Never gives anything away that he doesn't want to give away.'

'Have you considered that he may be Edward Gough or Perry St Martin?' asked Harris. 'Some kind of falling out with Graydon?'

'If Graydon ever existed.'

'You're not convinced?'

'We had started to wonder if the elusive tycoon act was all a front. That Gough and St Martin invented John Graydon to cover up their own dodgy dealings. The original team were unable to track down Graydon's family and there was none of the usual stuff you'd expect to find, National Insurance numbers, that sort of thing. And the home address for him at Companies House belonged to a garage in central Manchester that had been derelict for years.'

'Well, someone got onto the plane that afternoon.'

'They did and, as far as the staff at Prestwick were concerned, it was John Graydon with John Graydon's passport. Whoever he was, Passenger Eleven was as real as they come.' Armannsson hesitated. 'Look, don't get mad but those people who say your force is too small to handle an investigation like this? Our Chief Constable is one of them.'

'I know.'

'You heard it from Leckie, I assume?'

'Actually, no,' said Harris. 'As for your chief, I'm not surprised he said that about us. He and I did not exactly part on good terms.'

'There's a pattern emerging here, Jack. What happened?'

'He said the backwater thing to my face.' Harris gave a slight smile. 'Only once, mind. People don't say things like that to me twice.'

'I imagine they don't.'

There was a knock on the door and Matty Gallagher walked into the inspector's office.

'Sorry to interrupt,' he said, 'but the guy from the Air Accidents Investigation Branch has been on the blower. Turns out that he retired to a village at the far side of the valley.'

'Retired?' Harris did not look impressed.

'Yeah, High End, is it?' said Gallagher. 'Anyway, he reckons he'll be here just before two.'

'Well, retired or not, it will be good to get an expert take on things.'

'I wouldn't say that until you've met him,' replied Gallagher. 'He seems to have taken the news about a fresh investigation as some sort of personal affront.'

'Why?'

'Apparently, he was one of the team that wrote the final report.' The sergeant looked at Harris. 'Be warned, he is one prickly customer.'

'I think I can handle prickly, Matty lad.'

'If you can get a word in, guv. He's got a lot to say for himself has George Fenchurch. Damage to his reputation, blah, blah. Oh, another thing. The pilot? Ray Malahide? We have tracked down his wife. She lives in the Scottish Borders and Gillian suggested that she and I go to see her. Bit sensitive to do it on the phone.'

'Good idea,' said Harris. He waited for Gallagher to leave the room then looked at Armannsson. 'Hopefully, we can show your chief that he's wrong about us.'

'I wouldn't get too hopeful,' said Armannsson.

Chapter ten

A couple of minutes after Armannsson had left the inspector's office, there was a knock on the door and Danny Caulker walked in.

'Same old Jack Harris,' said the detective constable. 'You just can't resist blondes, can you?'

'My interest in your governor is entirely professional.' Harris gestured for Caulker to take a seat. 'Not that it's any of your business.'

Caulker sat down and glanced round at the cramped office.

'Hardly what I'd expect for a DCI,' he said.

'If you only came here to be rude…'

'No, no,' said Caulker. He held up his hands in mock-surrender. 'Didn't mean to cause trouble, Jack. Thought I ought to come and say that I have no problems working with you.'

'Surely it should be the other way round?' said Harris. 'It was you who deserted your post on that surveillance operation, remember.'

'Yes, but there was a reason…'

'There's never a reason for doing something like that.'

'Yes, but did you really have to…?'

'Look, Danny,' said Harris, leaning forward, 'you and I may have not got on back in Manchester but reporting you to the Super was nothing personal. I had no option. You not being there could have kyboshed everything. We could have lost the shipment, for a start. Not to mention the fact that you put an undercover officer at risk. You can thank your lucky stars that we got away with it.'

Caulker looked at the stern expression on the inspector's face. The constable sighed; everyone knew that you only ever came off second best in an encounter with an angry Jack Harris. And, although it hurt to admit it, Caulker knew that the DCI was right.

'I guess I *was* out of order,' he said grudgingly. It seemed the politic thing to say. 'That's why I'm here. Wanted you to know that you can trust me. And I'm sorry for what happened.'

Harris nodded.

'Fair enough,' he said. 'Let's say nothing more about it. What's your take on this little caper then? John Graydon still alive?'

'Not sure,' said Caulker; he was glad to talk about something else and relieved that Harris appeared to have accepted his apology. The constable had been dreading the encounter.

'What about your anonymous caller?' asked Harris. 'Is he right that the aircraft was sabotaged?'

'Not sure about that either,' said Caulker.

'None of you seem sure about anything.'

'I have my doubts, Jack. I did not meet Graydon but I knew St Martin and Gough from when I was starting out in Altrincham and I can't see them bringing a plane down. St Martin was a flash git but all mouth.'

'And Gough?'

'Very smooth. Salesman type. A fast talker. But they were nothing, a couple of young wannabees.'

'So maybe bringing the plane down was their way of hitting the big league?' said Harris.

Caulker shook his head.

'Can't see it,' he said. 'It's too big a leap for me.'

He hesitated.

'Go on,' said Harris. 'If there's something I need to know…'

'Look, between you and me, I'm worried that our chief can only see the headlines.' Caulker lowered his voice, even though they were alone in the room. 'He's only been in post for five months and Jenny got her job two weeks ago. I worry that they think they need a big score to make people accept them. Prove that they are up to the job. This is politics, Jack.'

Harris did not reply. He was beginning to think the same thing. And questioning his own motives. Wondering if the prospect of a major investigation had clouded his judgement. And yet… And yet…

Chapter eleven

'You were one of the original investigators into the air crash, I think?' said Jack Harris without much enthusiasm.

'I was the *senior* investigator,' said George Fenchurch tartly. 'I led the team and was the main author of the report.'

Fenchurch removed his black overcoat to reveal a dark blazer, a crisp white shirt with top button fastened and a tie bearing an RAF insignia. He was a lean man with close-cropped hair and tinges of black showing through the grey. George Fenchurch was one of those people in whom you could see their previous self. He sat down at the desk and Harris sighed as the retired investigator flicked an imaginary speck of dust off his trousers. Everything about his demeanour spoke of a rules man and one who resented being summoned to the police station.

The detective's mood was not improved when he saw his visitor scowl at the dogs, who were asleep in their customary position beneath the radiator. Jack Harris had never liked people who displayed a lack of empathy for animals.

'They let you keep them here?' asked Fenchurch.

'No.'

Fenchurch curled his lip in disdain.

'So,' he said. 'How can I assist your investigation?'

'If I am honest,' said the detective, 'I'm not sure you can. I was hoping that they would send us someone more impartial.'

'I was good enough for the Air Accidents Investigation Branch then and I am good enough for them now.' Fenchurch had bridled at the comment and his tone was defensive. 'Like I told your sergeant on the phone, if you go round suggesting that I am not impartial, I will have to take the matter up with your superior officer. Such comments impugn my reputation. A reputation, might I add, built up over many years.'

'To be honest, Mr Fenchurch, I've never been big on reputation.' Harris tried to adopt a more conciliatory tone. 'Besides, all I am saying is that you might not be the best placed person to…'

'Look, Chief Inspector,' snapped Fenchurch. 'I do not need to be here. I am only volunteering my time because the Branch thought that my knowledge of the case would prove useful to you. If all you are going to do is cast aspersions on my good name, then I can just as easily walk out of here.'

'I am not casting…'

'However, if you *do* want my opinion, I think that re-opening the inquiry is a complete waste of everyone's time. Mine included.'

'But is there not the possibility that you missed something first time around?'

'Of course we didn't miss anything, man!' Fenchurch glared at the inspector and, for a moment, the detective thought that he was going to carry out his threat and leave the room. Instead, the air investigator battled with his fury and remained seated. 'Others may have adopted a less conscientious approach to their work but not my team. I have investigated crashes all over the world and I am telling you that we conducted a thorough and highly professional inquiry into what happened here. I don't know what you hope to achieve by going over old ground.'

'There have been some recent developments.'

'I thought the skeleton was a hoax?'

'We are not investigating the skeleton. Some new information has come to light.'

'I would be highly surprised if it was anything to do with the crash. That was straightforward, as my report said. Pilot error. As clear a case as you could ever hope to encounter.'

'I am sure you are right...'

'Then why are you re-investigating it, for goodness' sake?'

'Because we have received information that the plane was sabotaged.'

'Who told you that?'

'An anonymous informant.'

'Poppycock!' Fenchurch's anger spilled out again. His cheeks flushed red and he jabbed the desk with his forefinger until the nail glowed white. 'Do you not think that a man of my experience would have spotted something like that?'

'Yes, but...'

'All you need to know is that Ray Malahide made an error of judgement and it cost fourteen people their lives. Unless you have some new evidence, I see no point in re-investigating the incident.' Fenchurch gave the detective a hard look. 'Have you got new evidence?'

Harris remained silent.

'I thought not,' snorted Fenchurch. 'Waste of bloody time!'

* * *

'There is no way that my husband made a mistake,' said the tearful grey-haired woman as she sat in the armchair and looked at Gillian Roberts and Matty Gallagher.

Patricia Malahide dabbed red-rimmed eyes with a lace handkerchief.

'I hope that you can put that right and restore his reputation,' she said. 'You have no idea the cruel things that people have said about him.'

She started to sob again. The detectives, who were sitting on the sofa in the trim living room of the semi-detached house in Melrose, waited for her to compose herself as they balanced tea in bone china cups on their knees.

'I know this is difficult,' said Roberts eventually. 'And we do not want to bring back painful memories...'

'Bring them back!' exclaimed Patricia. 'You have no idea what I have gone through! Not a minute goes by when I do not think of what happened to my poor Ray!'

'I'm sure,' said the detective inspector. She adopted her most tactful, motherly voice. 'And we appreciate that, Patricia. However, we cannot ignore the fact that the original inquiry concluded that the cause was pilot error.'

'That man!' The vehemence of Patricia's response startled the detectives. Spittle glistened on her lips as she glared angrily at them. 'It's all the fault of that bloody man!'

'What man?' asked Gallagher.

'George Fenchurch!' said Patricia. 'He had made up his mind before he even arrived at the crash site.'

'Why on earth would he do a thing like that?' said Gallagher.

'To get back at Ray, of course. They had never got on. Ray didn't rate him as a pilot and he told him so more than once. George had waited for years to pay him back.'

'I'm sure that's not the case,' said Roberts. 'From what we hear, George Fenchurch was a highly-respected investigator.'

'Yes, and didn't he like people to know it?' said Patricia bitterly. 'He deliberately set out to blacken my husband's name when he knew that he couldn't defend himself. He didn't have the courage to do it when Ray was alive.'

'How did they know each other?' asked Gallagher.

'They worked at the same airline after they came out of the RAF, before Ray went to work for the charter company. Ray was amazed when they made Fenchurch an air accident investigator.'

'Nevertheless,' said Gallagher, 'the report was pretty clear that your husband reacted too late to…'

'I know what it damn well said!' Patricia gave him a fierce look. 'Do you know how long my husband had been flying, Sergeant? Do you? Forty-one years, that's how long. Forty-one years without an accident! What happened to the plane was more likely to have been someone not doing their job properly at the charter company than something my Ray did. He always said that they cut corners.'

'Really?' Gallagher leaned forward in his seat. 'In what way?'

'Ray said that not all the checks were being done but the pilots got in trouble if they turned back. You have no idea the pressure that Howletts put their pilots under. Ray never liked it.'

'Then why did he work for them?' asked Gallagher.

'We needed the money. The boys needed help going through university. But Ray was never happy there.' She had calmed down a little. 'He said that they were always looking for ways to cut costs. I think that is why he ignored the fault – he said that things went wrong with their planes all the time.'

'Are you sure about all of this?' asked Roberts. 'The official report made no mention of that kind of thing happening.'

'And why do you think that is?' Patricia's anger was back. 'Because George Fenchurch was determined to pin all the blame on my husband, that's why. And because he succeeded, I did not get a penny's compensation.'

'We all get it wrong sometimes,' said Roberts. 'It's just that your husband did it at 20,000 feet.'

'Not my Ray.'

* * *

'Ray Malahide had grown sloppy,' said Fenchurch, looking across the desk at Harris. 'The man was making mistakes and, if you ask me, the charter company did not ask too many questions because he was prepared to work cheap. Howletts would not have got me for that salary, I can tell you.'

'But surely he was an experienced pilot?' said Harris. He pulled a sheet of paper out of a pile on the desk and scanned the contents. 'He'd been flying for forty-one years, it says here. And no accidents.'

'But there *had* been slip ups. He had just got lucky. Believe me, Chief Inspector, if I had wanted to, I could have said so much more about Ray Malahide in the final report.'

'Why didn't you then?'

'My job was to give my view on the cause of the accident, which is what I did. It would have been different if he had lived. It would have been my duty to see to it that Ray Malahide never flew again. Look, I know I may be coming over as harsh about a man who lost his life but it gives me no pleasure to say these things.' The anger had gone from Fenchurch, to be replaced by something softer. Sadder even. 'I don't know if you are aware, but we went way back. It's tragic what happened.'

'Weren't your bosses worried that your friendship would colour your investigation?'

'Oh, we were not friends, Chief Inspector. Far from it, but I had a reputation for scrupulous fairness. My managers knew that, whatever my opinion of Ray Malahide, my final report would be truthful. No, in my view, he let his standards slip when he went to work for Len Howlett's charter company. I think he thought he could get away with things because they weren't as rigorous.'

Harris picked up his copy of the air accident investigation report.

'And yet you said none of this,' he said. 'How come?'

'Because I don't blame Len or anyone at the company for what happened that night. The company might have been under pressure to keep costs down but I don't believe that they meant for pilots or ground crew to ignore problems. No, I think it was a genuine wiring fault that happened after the plane took off. Ray Malahide should have acted when he saw it but didn't.'

'Could not the altimeter have been sabotaged, though?'

'Anything is possible, I suppose,' said Fenchurch in a tone of voice that suggested that it wasn't.

'What about the mechanic?' The inspector reached for another piece of paper and scanned the contents. 'What did you make of him?'

'Good man,' said Fenchurch with an approving nod. 'If James Trewick said that the plane was good to go that afternoon, then it was good to go.'

'But it's still possible that he missed a problem, yes?'

'I'd be amazed if he did, Chief Inspector. If James Trewick was one thing, it was thorough.'

'And are you still prepared to take another look at the wreckage?'

'Under sufferance, because I would rather not leave my wife. She's not well. The wreckage is in a warehouse in Hertfordshire. I plan to go down tomorrow.'

'I'd like to accompany you.'

'I am not sure that is a good idea,' said Fenchurch. 'There are tens of thousands of pieces and it requires an expert eye to work out what is important and what is not.'

'Nevertheless, I think that someone from the police side of things should be present.'

'And are you versed in the ways of aircraft investigation?'

'Not as such. But I still want to go. Get a feel for things.'

Fenchurch shrugged.

'As you wish,' he said, standing up and putting on his coat. 'But I tell you now, I think it highly unlikely that I will come up with a different conclusion. I'll see myself out.'

After the investigator had gone, Harris glanced at the dogs.

'Come on, boys,' he said, standing up. 'Time for a walk. I need to have a think. Not least about who is going to look after you while I'm away.'

The inspector had just fished the leads out of his desk drawer when Philip Curtis walked in. Harris noted that the commander's customary disapproving expression in the direction of the dogs was identical to that displayed by George Fenchurch a few minutes earlier. The inspector sighed and sat back down.

'I assume that was the air crash investigator who passed me in the corridor?' said Curtis as he sat down at the desk.

'Was he chuckling in a jovial fashion?'

'Actually, he did not look very happy,' said Curtis.

'That's him.'

'I take it you and he did not get on then?'

'I do not like the man. Anyway, I've agreed to take him to Hertfordshire to see the wreckage tomorrow.'

'Really? This is nothing to do with a certain DCI who does not fancy spending all Friday night in a police car on an anti-burglary initiative, is it?'

Harris assumed an innocent expression.

'Who me?' he said.

* * *

Gallagher looked at Patricia Malahide.

'Please keep this to yourself,' he said, 'but what would you say if I told you that we have information that the flight was sabotaged?'

She looked shocked.

'Sabotaged?' she said. 'Who told you that?'

'An anonymous informant.'

'Well I know nothing about that.' However, a gleam had appeared in Patricia's eyes. 'But if it was true, that would mean that nothing Ray did would have saved those people, wouldn't it?'

'He'd still…'

'It would make Ray a victim of crime, wouldn't it? And if that was the case, could I not get compensation?'

'I would not like to say.'

The detectives stood up to leave.

'So, what happens now?' asked Patricia as she ushered them into the hallway. 'What will you do?'

'I am not sure,' said Roberts. 'The person who contacted the police in Manchester did not give them any information to support his claim.'

'And, whatever you think of George Fenchurch,' said Gallagher, 'the original investigation found nothing to suggest foul play.'

'But were they looking?' said Patricia. She grasped the sergeant's arm so tightly that he winced with the pain. 'Just clear my Ray's name!'

'We'll see what we can do,' said Gallagher. He loosened her grip. 'But we're not making any promises, Mrs Malahide. There's not a lot to go on.'

Chapter twelve

A couple of minutes after leaving Patricia Malahide's house, Roberts and Gallagher were sitting back in the sergeant's car.

'So, is she kidding herself?' asked Gallagher. He looked across to Roberts, who was fastening her seatbelt. 'Trying to tell herself that her beloved Ray didn't cause all those deaths? Mind, did you see the way she changed when she thought that she might get some money?'

'I did but we should not be too harsh. She *did* lose her husband.' Roberts looked over to the house where Patricia was watching them from the living room window, tears streaming down her face. 'Poor woman.'

'Maybe.'

'You're a hard man, Matthew Gallagher.'

Before either officer could speak further, and before Gallagher could turn on the vehicle's ignition, his mobile phone rang. It was Butterfield. He took the call and put it on speaker.

'You know you were looking for the guy who ran the charter company?' said the detective constable. 'Len Howlett? Well, we've found him and his workplace's not far from where you are at the moment. He's not very keen about it but he's agreed to see you if you want to pop in.'

'Is he still in aviation?' asked Gallagher.

'No, all the bad publicity following the crash meant that his company went bankrupt within a matter of weeks. No, these days, Len Howlett is an assistant manager in the bakery at a supermarket.'

'Now there's a career that never really took off,' said Gallagher.

'Funny guy,' said Butterfield.

The sergeant's phone rang again once he had stopped talking to Butterfield. Gallagher listened for a few moments, said 'cheers for keeping me in the loop' and rang off.

'Definitely not good for the CV,' said the sergeant.

'What do you mean?' asked Roberts.

'That was my mate in the National Crime Agency who's investigating where the skeleton came from. They've lifted the kids in Newcastle and they've all been suspended from their courses. Possible charges to follow.' He started the car's engine. 'Come on, let's go and see what our Mr Howlett has to say for himself.'

* * *

An hour later, Gallagher and Roberts were sitting amid the murmur of conversation and tinkle of crockery of the supermarket café, surveying the thin-faced man in the baker's hat and white coat who was sitting on the opposite side of the table. For his part, Len Howlett nursed a mug of tea and returned their gaze without much enthusiasm.

'I told your officer on the phone,' he said, 'I do not really have anything to add to what I said during the original inquiry. Why are you re-investigating the crash anyway?'

'We have received information that it was sabotage.'

'Of course it wasn't bloody sabotage!' exclaimed Howlett loudly. 'What a ridiculous thing to say!'

A few people at other tables looked over.

'You read the investigator's report,' said Howlett in a lower voice. He leaned towards them. 'It was down to pilot error. Plain and simple. The report said so.'

'We know what the report said,' replied Gallagher. 'But Patricia Malahide says that you cut corners.'

'That woman!' exclaimed Howlett, his voice rising again. People turned to look at him once more. 'She lets her mouth go far too much. She's embittered.'

'Maybe she has a right to be embittered,' said Roberts.

'She's a money-grabber. Her husband had not been dead two days before she was ringing me demanding compensation.'

'Yes, but she was a widow.'

'Maybe she was but a lot of people lost loved ones that night, Inspector. And don't forget that I lost my business as well. It was all I'd ever dreamed of doing, running my own charter company, and her bloody husband destroyed me.' Tears started in Howlett's eyes. 'Him and what he said in the black box recorder. Of course, we didn't order our pilots to ignore faults.'

'I app…'

'Do you have any idea what it was like following the crash?' said Howlett, his voice rising again. This time he ignored the looks from people on other tables. 'Do you? To have everyone blame you for killing all those people?'

'I can imagine,' said Roberts.

'I very much doubt it,' said Howlett. He lowered his voice again. 'People crossed the street to avoid talking to me. People I'd known for years. My wife left me and moved away because it got so bad. The kids were getting abuse in the playground and no one would give me a job after what happened. It took me ages to get work here.'

'And you've been here ever since?' asked Roberts, glancing over towards the aisles.

'Oddly enough, no one in aviation wants to employ someone whose plane crashed,' said Howlett bitterly.

'Tends not to inspire confidence. Look, Inspector, we did not cut corners, you can take it from me. James Trewick said that plane was fine to fly and I believe him. Who's told you it was deliberate anyway?'

'An anonymous informant,' said Gallagher.

'Well whoever it is, they're pulling your pud.' Howlett glanced at the wall clock, stood up and drained his mug. 'I have to go. We're short-handed today. Thanks for the tea.'

As the detectives watched him leave, Roberts' mobile rang. It was Harris. The inspector took the call as the detectives walked through the café in the direction of the exit.

'How's it going?' asked Harris. 'You seen Howlett yet?'

'Yeah, just. Seems to be more interested in covering his back than finding out what really happened.'

'George Fenchurch is the same. Says the original investigation got it right when it blamed Ray Malahide.'

'Maybe he's right. Although, I have to say that it is all very convenient that everyone is blaming someone who can't speak for himself.'

'Yeah,' said Harris. 'Funny that, eh?'

* * *

The mobile phone rang shortly after seven in the evening as Perry St Martin (although few people called him that these days) sat on a lounger, sipping a cool drink by the pool at his villa in Fuengirola on the Costa del Sol. He checked the identity of the caller before hitting the receive button. Just like he always did. You could not be too careful.

'What news?' asked St Martin.

'He's right,' said the voice on the other end. 'The cops *are* re-investigating the air crash.'

St Martin sat forward.

'Are you sure?' he asked sharply. 'There's been nothing about it on Sky. They just said the skeleton was a hoax.'

'I'm sure. My man confirmed it. Should we be worried?'

St Martin thought for a few moments, regained his composure then took another sip of his drink.

'No,' he said. 'Let them investigate. They failed last time and they'll fail this time. We covered our tracks.'

'But it's not just the Fraud Squad now, Perry.'

St Martin felt the first twinges of concern.

'What do you mean?' he asked, his glass halted half-way up to his mouth.

'They've linked up with the cops at Levton Bridge. The plane came down in their area, apparently.'

St Martin relaxed.

'That's OK,' he said. 'There's no way some woolly-back force can trace it back to us. It'll blow over soon enough. Once they realise that they're wasting their time.'

'Maybe it will, Perry, but they are asking a lot of questions. They're talking to Len Howlett and Patricia Malahide. And the word is that they are looking for James Trewick as well. They've got Fenchurch to check through all the wreckage. See if he missed anything. I tell you, this lot mean business.'

'So it would seem,' said St Martin grimly. 'Any idea who is leading the inquiry?'

'Some bloke called Harris. He's a DCI.'

St Martin felt the twinges return, stronger this time.

'Jack Harris?' he said.

'That's him,' said the caller. 'Used to be based in Manchester, apparently. You know him?'

'Only by reputation,' said St Martin.

'Look, if you think this Harris bloke can cause us trouble, maybe we should pay up.'

'I'm not doing that again,' said St Martin. 'I told you that last time, nobody plays me for a fool twice. No, leave it to me. I'll sort it. And don't ring me on this number again, right? I'll call you. And be careful. No stupid mistakes.'

'As ever, Perry.'

Once he had finished the call, Perry St Martin sat and thought for a few moments. He cursed beneath his breath and tossed the phone into the pool. He picked up another phone from the side table and dialled a number.

'You know a place called Levton Bridge,' he asked when a man answered.

'Never heard of it.'

'Well, check it up on Google maps. I've got a job for you. Something I need you to get for me.'

Chapter thirteen

As Jack Harris stood in the chill of the warehouse the following afternoon and stared at what remained of the charred and twisted wreckage of the aircraft, he knew exactly how the terrified passengers must have felt in the moments leading up to their deaths. Memories came flooding back for the inspector as he looked in solemn silence at the shards of metal and the ripped and scorched seats, visible through ugly gashes that had been torn in the fuselage by the force of the blast.

For the inspector, his memories were of another crash, of another stricken aeroplane, of another pilot struggling desperately to avoid ploughing into the ground in failing light. This plane was a military transport lumbering above the treetops as it carried a young Jack Harris and his fellow troops to a nearby base following a week of gruelling jungle survival training in Belize.

All was gloom in the cabin as the soldiers sat in silence, exhausted by their week's exertions in the sweltering forest. Any attempts at conversation had long since ended, the troops' voices drowned out by the monotonous clatter of the propellers. Eyes glowed white in the half-light and skin glistened with grime and sweat as the plane made its way across the jungle. None of the soldiers were sad to leave it behind, certainly not Private Jack Harris; he had always prided himself on his fitness but he had found the experience more demanding than anything he had ever done. Now, he sat with his eyes closed and tried to ignore the pain from a myriad of insect bites and from aching limbs that had been tested to their limit by the instructors.

After half an hour, one of the engines coughed and the plane shook and started to slow as one of the propellers cut out.

'What the fuck?' exclaimed one of the soldiers as the aircraft started to lose height and the remaining engine began to roar.

It was all over very quickly. Smoke billowed from the damaged engine and the aircraft dipped and brushed the treetops as the pilot struggled to regain control.

'We're going down!' he shouted.

With a splintering of timber and a tearing of leaves, the transport ploughed into the forest canopy, smashing its way through the trees until it burst into a clearing where it slid along the ground, hurling up clouds of dirt until it came to a sudden and juddering halt when its nose struck a large rock, sending shockwaves coursing through the fuselage. Inside the plane, the troops had been hurled around the cabin during the descent and now men lay with blood oozing from wounds and limbs twisted at sickening angles. All was silence for a few moments, then there was groaning and screaming and panic.

Recovering his senses, Jack Harris reached down to gingerly feel his fractured ankle and winced with the pain. Looking closer, he could see that the bone was protruding through the sock and he felt his stomach heave. For a few moments, he felt as if he would pass out. Once the nausea had passed and his head had cleared, Harris looked around to see how his comrades had fared. That was when he saw the first dead man, a sergeant whose lifeless eyes stared out of a torn and blood-soaked face. Even though Jack Harris had been serving in the army for the best part of two years, for the young private it was the first experience of death.

The corpse was soon followed by more. As Harris struggled along the cabin, gritting his teeth against the pain from his ankle, he saw that three other troops were dead, and when he made his way into the *cockpit, he found the dead pilots, both with faces cut to ribbons by shards of glass. The young soldier felt his stomach heave again and he rushed out into a jungle that had fallen strangely silent.*

Crouched on the ground, vomit dribbling down his chin, Harris looked up to see, on the far side of the clearing, the broken body of his Captain, the man whose kindness had helped the young soldier adapt to life in the army. The captain had been hurled through a gaping hole ripped in the fuselage when the plane first hit the ground.

Never a day went by that Jack Harris did not at some point remember his Captain's mangled face. It was the first thing he had thought of when staring into the face of the skeleton on the hillside. Standing in the warehouse now, the inspector remembered his friend and felt a dull throbbing sensation in his ankle.

'Chief Inspector,' said a voice from afar. It seemed to echo. 'Are you alright?'

With a start, Harris was wrenched back to the present and a cold warehouse on a non-descript industrial estate on the edge of Stevenage. George Fenchurch was watching him with a knowing look on his face.

'Memories?' said the investigator.

'Something like that,' grunted the inspector.

'It never leaves you, does it?'

'What?'

'It never leaves you if you have experienced something like that,' said Fenchurch.

'And how would you know?' said Harris irritably.

'Because it happened to me. Aden, it was. My first posting abroad. I ejected after an engine problem. The plane hit a bus. Six people were killed.'

Harris cursed inwardly at the way that he had allowed himself to show weakness. Jack Harris had always abhorred weakness, detested it in himself and disliked it in others, and the last thing he wanted was to display vulnerability in front of George Fenchurch, a man whose air of superiority had increasingly irritated the detective on the journey south in the Land Rover that morning.

It had not been an enjoyable drive and, after trying to make forced conversation for an hour or so, the men had fallen silent somewhere in Yorkshire and had spoken little for the remainder of the trip. Ever since they had arrived at the warehouse shortly after 2pm, they had maintained a distant, but professional courtesy and now Harris found himself wrongfooted by the investigator. The inspector did not like the sensation.

'When was yours?' asked Fenchurch.

Don't give him the satisfaction, thought Harris, but was acutely conscious that Fenchurch was staring expectantly at him. Demanding an answer.

'Belize,' said Harris. 'Troop plane.'

The inspector hoped that his reply would suffice, would bring the conversation to an end, let them get on with the job in hand.

'I remember it.' Fenchurch shook his head. 'Nasty business. That one was pilot error as well. He let the engine stall, I seem to recall.'

'I'm not sure about that.'

'Well, it's true,' said Fenchurch. 'Perhaps they didn't let you grunts see the accident report but I saw it. They used it in training for the Branch. Take it from me, he made a mistake. Do you wish to talk about it? I never felt the need myself but I am told that it helped some of my colleagues when things like that happened. The less robust ones.'

Harris glared at him.

'No,' he said. 'I'm fine.'

'Sure?'

Harris found himself wishing that Gillian Roberts was there; he suspected that if the detective inspector had asked the same question, his answer would have been very different. That he *would* have talked about it for the first time in many years. Now he came to think about it, for the first time ever. However, the detective was not about to open himself up to George Fenchurch. This felt like a battle of wills and Jack Harris was in no mood to cede ground to his adversary. For Harris, control had always been everything. The inspector sensed that Fenchurch expected a reply.

'Yes, I'm sure,' said Harris. 'Can we get on with it?'

'As you wish.'

Harris let his gaze roam over the wreckage then across to the dozens of crates piled up in the corner of the warehouse, each one of them containing fragments of wreckage. He tried to sound business-like. Controlled.

'So, what are we looking for exactly?' he said.

'The same thing as last time.' Fenchurch walked over to the fuselage and ran a hand idly over one of the tears. 'Scotch mist. I'm telling you now, Chief Inspector, you won't find anything.'

'We might.'

'There is no way that the accident was sabotage.' Fenchurch shook his head with an exaggerated sense of frustration, as if to emphasise the point. 'However, no one seems to be listening.'

'But, as investigators, should we not keep an open mind?'

The inspector felt a need to regain the initiative and was struggling once again to control the desire to tell Fenchurch precisely what he thought of him. He had already shown uncharacteristic restraint because he knew that, like it or not, George Fenchurch had been put forward by the Air Accidents Investigation Branch as its official representative. Philip Curtis' last words before Harris had left the police station the previous evening were that the inspector would have to respect Fenchurch's status, regardless of whether or not he liked the man.

'I mean,' continued Harris. He tried to sound as respectful as he could but inevitably his irritation showed through. 'What if you made a mistake?'

'Me, make a mistake?' Fenchurch appeared surprised by the suggestion. 'I hardly think so, Chief Inspector.'

'But how can you be sure? I mean, you haven't been able to examine the altimeter for a start, have you?' Harris gestured to the boxes piled up in the corner of the warehouse. 'It's still missing, is it not? It's not in any of them as far as we know.'

Harris walked over to him; the inspector was a big man and he hoped that proximity would intimidate Fenchurch. The tactic did not work.

'It is missing, yes,' said Fenchurch. He calmly returned the inspector's gaze. 'But given the state it will be in after twenty years buried in mud, I think it highly unlikely that it could tell us much, even if we did find it.'

Fenchurch gestured at the wreckage.

'No, this is what pilot error looks like,' he said. 'You, of all people, should recognise that.'

Before Harris could reply, his phone rang. He looked down at the screen and took the call.

'Matty lad,' said the inspector.

'How's it going with Cuddles?' asked the sergeant.

'Marvellous,' said Harris sourly. He walked across the warehouse so that Fenchurch could not eavesdrop on their conversation. 'Much more of this and I'll give the sanctimonious bastard a slap.'

'I thought Curtis told you to be on your best behaviour.'

'Sod that for a game of soldiers. You were right, the man's a right royal pain in the backside. You making any progress at your end?'

'We're working our way through the families of those who died in the crash,' said Gallagher. 'We're really stirring things up, guv. We've got a lot of upset people on our hands. None of them buy the sabotage theory, though. They all blame Ray Malahide.'

'Doesn't everybody?'

'So, it would seem,' said the sergeant. 'Oh, and we've tracked down the mechanic who oversaw the checks on the plane. James Trewick. Lives near Glasgow.'

'You talked to him yet?'

'Only on the phone,' replied Gallagher. 'He says that he has nothing to add to what he told Fenchurch at the time.'

'I take it that he doesn't buy the sabotage theory either, then?'

'Not at all. He says it would be impossible for anyone to tamper with the plane without him knowing. He goes with Fenchurch's idea that it was a wiring fault that occurred once they were in the air. Something working loose. Planes often hit a patch of turbulence as they arrive at the North Pennines, apparently.'

'Yes, but they don't all crash, do they?' said Harris. 'You think it's worth going to see him?'

'Be nice to look him in the eyes, see if he's lying. He's very unwell, mind – COPD, in and out of hospital – so he's reluctant to see us. You want me to press him anyway?'

'Please.'

'It may not be for a day or two if we do get to see him,' said Gallagher. 'He's been pretty bad this week and he's got a couple of hospital appointments. From what his wife said, he might not have all that long.'

'We have to see him, though, Matty lad. Take Gillian with you. You'll need someone to make sure you're OK.'

'Eh?'

'You have never gone that far north, have you? Who knows what effect it might have on your metabolism?'

Gallagher laughed; another joke from his boss.

'I have gone that far, actually,' he said. 'Chelsea played Celtic in a pre-season friendly a few years back and me and some of the lads from Bermondsey Nick went up to Glasgow for the weekend. Crap fish and chips, as I recall. It was worth it, mind, Chelsea battered them.'

Gallagher paused to allow Harris to laugh at his joke but the inspector remained silent.

'Did you get it?' said the sergeant. 'Battered. Fish and chips?'

'I got it.'

'I'm wasted on you, I really am,' said Gallagher. 'How long you staying down there then? You and Fenchurch going to get a room together?'

'I was thinking of coming back tomorrow but can you send someone else down first? We should have someone on hand to make sure that Fenchurch doesn't try to worm out of it before he's finished. Send Alistair Marshall. The experience will do him good.'

'Will do. Talk later.'

'Anything interesting?' asked Fenchurch as the inspector walked back towards the fuselage, slipping the phone into his coat pocket as he did so.

'My sergeant has tracked down James Trewick,' said Harris.

'Did he confirm what I said?'

'Word for word.'

'I thought he would.' Fenchurch gestured to the wreckage. 'I take it you know that this will take days to check?'

'Has to be done.'

'Are you really sure about that? I'm not happy about leaving Elizabeth this long. She really is not well. Looks like she's going to have to go into a nursing home.'

'Then we had better get started, hadn't we?' said Harris.

Fenchurch scowled. Harris smiled inwardly. Control, he thought.

* * *

Gallagher had just returned to the police station and was making a cup of tea in the squad room when his desk phone rang.

'Sergeant Gallagher,' he said into the receiver.

'Sergeant Gallagher?' said the voice of Patricia Malahide. 'I've just remembered something about the crash.'

Gallagher sat down and reached for his notepad.

'What's that then?' he asked.

'Something Ray said once. He said that it would be easy for a mechanic to sabotage an aircraft without anyone knowing.'

'And did he have any evidence of that having ever happened?'

'No, but it's interesting, isn't it? Maybe you should talk to James Trewick.'

'Maybe we should,' said Gallagher. 'Thank you for ringing.'

The sergeant ended the call and scratched out the note he had been starting to write.

'Money,' he said. 'Always money.'

Chapter fourteen

Just before 4.30pm, Danny Caulker's mobile phone rang as he walked into the room on the first floor of Levton Bridge Police Station allocated to the Manchester Fraud Squad team. Seated at desks by the window, Armannsson and Leckie watched as Caulker listened to the person on the other end of the call, occasionally grunting but saying little.

Leckie glanced out of the window; if he stared across the rooftops hard enough, he could just make out the faint outline of the hills, now shrouded by mist in the gathering late afternoon gloom that was once more settling on the valley. The constable sighed and thought of Hawk and their delayed fishing trip. God knows when they'd get round to it now.

Caulker finished the call.

'That was the office,' he said. 'Our informant has been on again. Said he had heard that we are reinvestigating the plane crash.'

'How did he know?' asked Armannsson. 'We've not issued anything to the media and I sure as hell didn't tell him when he rang last time.'

'Folks get to hear these things, don't they? And Harris's lot *have* been asking a lot of questions. Anyway, our guy is still adamant that John Graydon is in the Cayman Islands.'

'And the others?' asked Armannsson. 'Gough and St Martin? Is he prepared to tell us where they are yet? Does he even know?'

'If he does, he's not saying.' The detective constable went over to the kettle and looked at the others. 'Brew, anyone?'

They both nodded and he switched the kettle on and reached three mugs down from the overhead cupboard.

'Perhaps our guy really is playing games with us,' said Caulker. He turned round with a box of teabags in his hand. 'There's been a lot of conspiracy theories with the twentieth anniversary coming up. Maybe he's just another crackerjack. What do you think, Graham? Loony?'

'Possibly. Your informant has not been telling us anything we could not have guessed for ourselves, has he? Graydon in the Cayman Islands? He wouldn't be the first to hide out there, would he? Plane sabotaged? Well, it has been reported often enough that the altimeter is missing and what else has he told us? Just vague statements. As for knowing that we are re-investigating the crash, perhaps he saw all the cops and worked it out. Wouldn't take a genius.'

'But someone moved Graydon's cash,' said Armannsson.

'So back to your first theory then. Graydon panicked. And our informant has not mentioned that, so he clearly doesn't know everything, does he?'

Armannsson shook her head.

'No,' said Leckie, warming to his theme, 'at the moment, a very expensive police operation has been launched on the word of an anonymous informant with nothing to back up what he is telling us.'

It was Armannsson's turn to stare gloomily out of the window as the clouds gathered over the valley. *How could*

Jack Harris love living in a place like this? she asked herself. She felt a sudden craving for the busy streets of Manchester. She noticed that the others were waiting for her to say something.

'Jack and his team really do need to turn up that altimeter,' she said.

'I wouldn't hold out too much hope,' said Leckie. 'It's the proverbial needle in the haystack. You'd be amazed what's buried out there. Stuff just sinks into the peat, never to be seen again. Hawk is still waiting for his Auntie Ethel to resurface after the picnic incident.'

Armannsson allowed herself a smile.

'Maybe Jack can find something in Stevenage then,' she said. 'God knows we need it.'

Her mobile phone rang. She listened to the person on the other end, jotted something down on a piece of paper and ended the call. Before she could speak, her phone rang again. Harris. She took the call.

'How's it going?' she asked.

'Not great,' replied Harris.

'Any sign of the altimeter?'

'I am pretty sure it's not here,' said Harris.

'When you coming back?'

'First thing tomorrow.'

'Fancy dropping in on Warwickshire on your way? Our office has just been on; they have tracked down the secretary from Graydon's company. Miriam Jacques.'

'Yeah, will do. Text me the details. Anything else?'

Armannsson hesitated.

'Look, don't get mad,' she said eventually, 'but we're beginning to wonder if our anonymous caller is making it all up.'

Harris looked across to the far side of the warehouse to where George Fenchurch was picking through shards of wreckage in a half-hearted manner.

'Now you tell me,' he said.

* * *

That night in the B and B, Jack Harris was jolted awake at 2am by a dream in which the troop carrier ploughed into the jungle. Once again, the young solder stumbled out of the wrecked cabin and into the clearing, to be confronted by the sight of his dead Captain, lifeless eyes staring out of a crushed face. As the detective lay in his bed, bathed in sweat and waiting for his heart to stop pounding, he struggled to banish the image. It was only when the first streaks of dawn began to filter through the curtains that the detective finally slipped back into a brief and fitful sleep.

Chapter fifteen

Jack Harris guided the Land Rover into the attractive Warwickshire village shortly after 10.30am and brought the vehicle to a halt outside a large detached house set in immaculately landscaped wooded gardens. He could see through the trees a large lawn, complete with pergola and a pond on the banks of which stood several stone statues of nymphs. The inspector drove up the drive, his tyres crunching on the gravel, and parked behind a new 4x4, glistening in the sharp morning sun.

'Nice,' he murmured.

As he walked towards the house, the front door swung open and an attractive, dark-haired woman watched him approach. The records suggested that she was sixty-one but she looked younger. Much younger.

'Miriam Jacques?' said the detective.

'That's me. You must be Mr Harris.'

'The very same.'

Miriam offered him her hand to shake. Harris noted that the grip was weak, different to the confident image that she was presenting. She ushered him into the large hallway where she studied the warrant card that he had held up.

'A detective chief inspector,' she said. 'I'm flattered. The last time this happened, the Fraud Squad only sent a couple of young constables.'

'So I gather.' Harris glanced along the hallway and noticed the expensive vase sitting on an occasional table and the original painting hanging at the top of the ornate staircase. 'Impressive house.'

'Thank you.' She ushered him into the spacious living room. 'Although, I fear that you have had a wasted journey, Chief Inspector. As I told your colleagues twenty years ago, I am not sure that I can be of much assistance. I know nothing about any missing money.'

Five minutes later, the inspector was sitting on a plush sofa while Miriam fussed over a tray of tea and biscuits which she had placed on a low glass table. Harris looked round at the expensive paintings lining the wall and the high-quality antique furniture. As Miriam handed him a bone china cup and saucer, she noted his interest and gave a knowing smile.

'It's not what you are thinking,' she said. 'It's not been paid for by John Graydon.'

'I wasn't thin…'

'Oh, come now, Inspector.' She sat down in an armchair and eyed him keenly. 'I saw on the news that you thought he had turned up. Even though it turned out to be a hoax, I did wonder if it might re-kindle interest in the case. Why else you would you make such a long journey?'

Harris held up his hands.

'Mea culpa,' he said.

'All this.' She waved a hand. 'All this is perfectly explainable. My husband was a stockbroker before he retired. I'm a widow now.'

'I'm sorry…'

'But only to golf.'

'Ah.' Harris took a sip of tea. 'Never seen the attraction, myself.'

'It keeps him from getting under my feet.'

'I'm sure it does,' said Harris. 'You were the secretary for Graydon Projects, I think?'

'For eighteen months, yes. They had an office in central Manchester. I was living in the city at the time.'

'What was John Graydon like?'

'I did not have much to do with him really. Whenever he came in, he locked himself away in meetings with the others.'

'That would be Edward Gough and Perry St Martin?'

'That's them.' She reached for a biscuit. 'As for John, he was nothing to look at. Mid-thirties, well dressed, quite charming in his own way. Very polite. Most of my dealings were with Edward and Perry, though.'

'And what were they like?'

'Very different.' Miriam frowned. 'To tell you the truth, you have stirred up a lot of unpleasant memories.'

'Like what?'

'There was something about them.' She gave him an unhappy look. 'I didn't really trust them. Particularly not Perry. Edward tended to do as he was told.'

Miriam paused, appearing to struggle with her bad memories. Harris said nothing, giving her the time that she needed to gather her thoughts.

'They were too flashy, that's what it was,' said Miriam at last. 'They wore the best suits, drove the biggest cars, had the most expensive jewellery.'

Harris glanced at the furniture and the paintings, thought of the 4x4 parked on the drive, but said nothing. Miriam seemed not to have noticed the irony in her comment. Instead, she seemed eager to unburden herself, almost as if she was uttering the words for the first time.

'They were not nice people, Inspector,' she said; the words were coming in a rush now. 'The way they spoke about people was very unpleasant. They were very disparaging about women. And they said offensive things about our investors behind their backs. One of them had a speech impediment and Perry was always mimicking him. I didn't like that.'

'Did you ever suspect that they were crooked?'

'I did wonder.' Even though they were alone in the house, she lowered her voice. 'They seemed to feed off each other. It wasn't healthy. Look, I shouldn't say this, but I was a little bit scared.'

Harris leaned forward.

'Scared?' he said. 'Why were you scared, Miriam?'

'Because of some of the people who came to the office. They were different from the investors. Rough types. Nasty men, I always thought. I'm pretty sure that some of them were criminals. And the way that Edward and Perry talked to them, it was obvious that they knew them.'

'Can you remember any names? Describe any of them?'

'I was just a secretary.' She took a sip of tea and Harris noticed that the hand holding the cup was trembling slightly. 'Besides, I do not think it would have been very wise to take too much of an interest. Then or now.'

'So, you've not heard from them since the plane crash?'

'No. And I do not wish to either. Look, why are you dragging all this up again?' She gave him an exasperated look. 'John Graydon is dead and I don't know what happened to Gough and St Martin.'

'We have been told that Graydon is living in the Cayman Islands.'

'Really?' Her surprise appeared to be genuine. 'Then who died in the plane crash?'

'We're not sure. Any help you can give us would be greatly appreciated. The office closed down very quickly after the crash, I think?'

'It did, yes. Myself and Eleanor – she did the payroll, died last year – we went back to the office the day after it happened but the landlord had already changed the locks. Said they owed him five thousand pounds in rent. From what I heard, they left a lot of unpaid bills.'

'And you have no idea where Gough and St Martin went?'

Miriam shrugged.

'Who knows?' she said. 'The police said they might be in Spain.'

'Do you know anything about their families? We're struggling to track them down.'

'Edward had a sister. She came to the office one day. Laura, I think she was called. Laura Mayhew. Not sure about the others. They never mentioned anyone. Look, I only took the job because I needed the money. The year after it all happened, I met Gerald and everything changed. I have no desire to re-live those days.' She looked at him defiantly; she had clearly decided that the interview was at an end. 'Will that be all?'

'One last thing. Did you ever hear anything that made you think that the plane crash was caused deliberately?'

She looked shocked. 'I heard nothing like that, Inspector. Unpleasant as they were, I cannot see any of them doing something like that. Can you?'

'I am not sure that I can, Miriam.' Harris drained his cup and stood up. Thanks for the tea.'

'I wish I could say it was a pleasure.'

* * *

Once she had watched the Land Rover reverse out of the drive and disappear in the direction of the motorway, Miriam walked over to her sideboard and opened a drawer, from which she took an address book. Flicking through the pages, she stopped at the letter 'S' and stood staring at the number for a few moments, deep in thought. Mind made up, she walked into the hall to the table bearing the house phone. She dialled a number. The call was answered by a man.

'Perry?' she said.

'I told you not to ring me again.'

'I know, but the police have been here. A detective called Jack Harris.'

'And what did you tell him?'

'That I do not know anything.'

'Yes, well, just keep it that way,' said St Martin. 'After all, we don't want to have to tell the saintly Gerald that you spent our money on men young enough to be your grandsons, do we? Not sure that fits in with his world view.'

'You can rely on me,' she said quickly.

'I hope, for your sake, that you are right, Miriam.'

* * *

As Jack Harris was guiding the Land Rover out of the village, his smartphone rang. Putting it on speaker, Harris took the call.

'Gillian,' he said. 'How goes it?'

'Slow to non-existent,' said Roberts. 'It feels like we've reached a dead-end.'

Harris thought of George Fenchurch picking his way through aircraft wreckage in the warehouse and of Miriam Jacques standing on the doorstep, with her arms crossed, as she watched the inspector depart.

'You could well be right,' he said. 'Before we give it up as a bad job, can you check a name out for me, please?'

He turned the vehicle in the direction of the northbound motorway. An hour and a half into his journey, his phone rang again. Private number.

'Harris,' said the inspector.

'DCI Harris?' said a woman's voice. 'My name is Laura Mayhew. I think you want to talk about my brother?'

Chapter sixteen

It was mid-afternoon when Jack Harris eventually took the Land Rover off the northbound M6 and made for the eastern fringes of the Lake District. After a few miles travelling on minor roads, he arrived at a sign that advertised a commercial stables and pointed the way up a winding drive to a large detached white house standing in its own landscaped grounds. Getting out of the vehicle outside the house, Harris stretched his right leg to ease the stiffness after all the driving, sniffed the crisp, fresh air and looked appreciatively at the hills with their snow-capped summits. His gaze roamed across to the range of stables and paddocks.

'Now this is more like it,' he said.

The door to the house was opened by a slim woman in her late forties. She smiled a welcome. Within minutes, Harris was sitting at the kitchen table, sipping at tea from a mug and enjoying a slice of home-made cake.

'Were you close to your brother?' asked Harris. He licked his fingers. 'This is excellent cake, by the way.'

'Thank you. It was my grandmother's recipe. I could tell you what's in it but I'd have to kill you afterwards.

And, presumably, one of your colleagues would have to come to arrest me.'

Harris smiled. There was something refreshing about the openness of Laura Mayhew after all the lies and evasive behaviour that he had encountered over recent days.

'You were going to tell me about Edward,' he said.

'We weren't really that close. We were as kids, growing up here. Absolutely inseparable. My dad always hoped that we would take over the business together when he retired but my brother had other ideas. He couldn't wait to get away.'

'I'm not sure that I'd ever want to leave here.'

'Well, Eddie did. Fell in with the wrong crowd when he was a teenager. Some lads from the village who were into drugs. Made him realise that there was more to life.'

'A common enough story,' said Harris. He did not mention that, as a teenager growing up in Levton Bridge, it had been *his* story. That it had been the reason he joined the Army. To escape bad influences and avoid taking the route that Edward Gough had followed.

'He spent some time in youth custody,' continued Laura. 'They broke into a couple of houses in the village to get money to buy heroin.'

'So I heard.'

She looked quizzically at him.

'Greater Manchester Police told me,' he said.

She nodded. Her demeanour had changed, taken over by a deep sense of regret.

'Things were awful when he came out,' she said quietly. 'He and Dad fought all the time. That's why Eddie ended up going to Manchester. They had a furious row the day he left and Eddie struck Dad. After he'd gone, Dad was in tears and he never saw Eddie again. He never came back here and Dad refused to go looking for him.'

'A sad story. And I'm sorry for making you tell it again after all these years.' Harris took a sip of tea and a bite of cake. 'Do you know how your brother came to meet up with John Graydon and Perry St Martin?'

'Not any of the details, I am afraid. Eddie's life was a bit of a mystery after that. All we heard from one of the lads in the village was that he'd fallen in with some bad people and didn't want to see us. Look, Chief Inspector, I'm not a fool, I know that my brother was no angel but he wasn't like the others. Especially Perry St Martin. I didn't like him at all.'

'You went to their office, I think?'

'Yes.' She looked surprised. 'How do you know that?'

'The secretary told us. Miriam Jacques.'

'No secrets in your world.'

'Too many,' said Harris. 'Why did you go to the office?'

'I was in Manchester for a conference and rang Eddie on the off-chance. I didn't expect him to answer, he never had before, but he said he wanted to show me where he worked. He was really proud of them.'

'But you didn't like Perry St Martin?'

'No, I didn't,' she said. 'There was something about the way he looked at me. Like he was undressing me with his eyes.'

'And Graydon?'

'He was a bit better. Quite likeable really. Look, what is this about, Chief Inspector?'

'I'll explain in a moment. You have not heard from Edward since the crash?'

'No. I just assumed that he was ignoring us again. After it happened, it all came out about the fraud and that Perry St Martin and my brother had disappeared because the police were after them. The fraud squad officer who came to see us said he thought that they may have gone to Spain.'

'You were interviewed?' It was the inspector's turn to look surprised. 'There's no record of that.'

'The detective did not seem that interested. Seemed more interested in the horses, actually. I never heard from

103

him again and we've not heard from Eddie since.' Tears glistened in her eyes. 'The longer we didn't hear from him, the more depressed my father became. He was dead within the year. Took sleeping pills. We found him in one of the stables. There was no note but I knew.'

'I'm sorry. Truly I am.' Harris gave her time to recover her composure. 'Do you think that your brother *is* in Spain?'

'If he is, he has never contacted any of the family.' She frowned. 'I know it sounds an awful thing to say but I always wondered if he might be dead. Look, are you going to explain what this is about?'

'We have information that John Graydon is alive.'

'Then who died on...?' She gave a little gasp. 'You think that it might have been Eddie?'

'We're not quite sure yet.' Harris hesitated. 'Look, I know this may be upsetting to hear, Laura, but there's a possibility that the crash may have been caused deliberately.'

'By Perry St Martin?'

Harris looked surprised again.

'What makes you say that?' he asked.

'There was something about the man.' A fierce expression came into Laura Mayhew's eyes. 'I could believe anything of Perry St Martin. Really I could.'

Chapter seventeen

The following day, shortly after three in the afternoon and with rain driving against the office window out of a leaden North Pennines sky, Philip Curtis looked across his desk at Jack Harris and Jenny Armannsson. The gloom outside was matched by the atmosphere in the room; both detectives knew what was coming. Although it was a decision that threatened to make them lose face in the eyes of sceptical colleagues, it was not one that either officer felt they could contest with any sense of conviction.

'I'm sorry,' said the district commander, 'but I really cannot see where this is going. Jenny, with the benefit of hindsight, we should have treated your informant with more circumspection. I think we all got carried away. Is that a fair comment, Jack?'

'It's fair enough,' said the inspector. 'There may be something there but I've heard nothing that justifies all the manpower we're expending on it. The most strident person is Patricia Malahide and she's only in it for the compensation.'

'So, go on then,' said Curtis. He looked expectantly at Armannsson. 'You're the one who brought this to us. Both chief constables are having second thoughts, as am I. Convince me that we are wrong to scale things back.'

Armannsson glanced at Harris to see if the inspector was going to say anything to assist her cause, but he stayed silent. She sighed; it was as she had suspected for a while – Jack Harris was regretting his initial decision to back her. Leckie had warned her at the outset that, if you played games with Harris, you had to be sure of your facts and the suspicion that the informant was a hoaxer had always been nagging away at the back of her mind. Now it was her turn to do the regrets, to regret the way she had allowed her eagerness to please her chief constable override everything else.

'Well?' said Curtis as the silence lengthened. 'Any argument?'

Armannsson shook her head.

'I can't say anything, sir,' she said.

'I thought so,' said Curtis. His tone softened. 'Look, I know this is disappointing for you – for both of you. Jack, I can maybe let you have another day or two if you think you need them.'

'I don't think we will,' said Harris. 'It's possible that we could even close the case today if things go the way we think they will.'

'And that just leaves the kids who made the film?'

'Yeah but we're not expecting the CPS to get heavy about it,' said Harris. 'It's much more about what the National Crime Agency decide to do about the skeleton. They've already bailed the lads. The girl is still helping them.'

'Well, the sooner we wash our hands of things, the better,' said Curtis. 'We are worried that the media may have got hold of the story. There's already been some speculation on social media and the press office has had a number of enquiries. I would be happier if we could shut everything down now.'

Harris nodded; he had never liked doing his job under media scrutiny. Jack Harris preferred to do things his way and had never welcomed the presence of prying journalists. For her part, Armannsson stared bleakly out of the office window at the grey sky and tried not to think what her Chief Constable would say, what her critics back in Manchester would say when she returned to the city. Earlier that day, she had walked into the corridor and caught Danny Caulker talking in hushed tones on his phone. He had loudly changed the subject when he saw her approaching but Jenny knew exactly what he was doing. She had known right from the off that Danny Caulker had little respect for her abilities and now she had given him and his friends all the ammunition they needed.

The detective inspector glanced across at Harris again. She had been trying to work out whether or not he blamed her for putting him in this position with his commander but he had rebuffed her attempts to discuss the matter whenever she raised the issue. Now, as so often, his face offered no clue as to what he was thinking and, in that moment, Jenny Armannsson felt more alone than she had ever felt. Harris noticed her discomfort and gave her the slightest of winks. It only lasted a fraction of a second but to Armannsson it meant everything.

* * *

Matty Gallagher and Gillian Roberts sat in the living room of the terraced house and looked bleakly at the man in the mask, who was slumped in an armchair. Sitting nearby on the floor was a large oxygen cannister. James Trewick was only in his mid-fifties but his grey pallor, and the way that his skin glistened with a sheen of sweat as he fought for breath, made him look older. Much older. He was, the detectives could clearly see, a man close to death. Trewick's wife sat on an armchair, all worries and lines, and the atmosphere in the room was oppressive.

'My husband really is not up to this,' she said. 'As you can see, he is very ill.'

'We appreciate that,' said Gallagher. 'We'll try to get through things as quickly as we can.'

'I still don't...'

'It's alright, Margaret,' said Trewick. The voice trembled and the breath wheezed in his lungs as he struggled to speak. 'Just give me a few moments.'

For a moment, it looked as if Margaret was going to object but she said nothing and stared unhappily out of the window onto the small but neat back garden. After a few moments, she looked back to her husband and her eyes glistened with tears.

As the former mechanic built up the strength to speak again, Gallagher looked at the pictures lined up on the sideboard. They portrayed James Trewick in happier days, at his son's university graduation, on his wedding day, grinning as he stood with other mechanics in front of a gleaming jet on a runway. The sergeant, whose years in the job had hardened him to most human suffering, found himself surprised by his reaction to the images, an overwhelming sense that the detectives were intruding on an acutely private agony.

Glancing across at Roberts, he saw that the detective inspector was watching Trewick's battle for breath with a mixture of pity and unease. Gallagher had been experiencing similar thoughts throughout the inquiry, as if the police were scratching at old wounds for no good reason. The sergeant had become convinced that the fraud squad's informant was nothing more than a sick hoaxer. If only he could see James Trewick now, thought Gallagher darkly. Then, perhaps, he would understand the damage that his words were causing.

'You are wasting your time,' said Trewick eventually. 'I told you on the phone, that plane was OK to fly. Whatever happened to make the altimeter play up happened after the aircraft left the hangar.'

He paused for breath. The detectives again gave him the time he needed. Again, it seemed as if his wife was going to protest but she stayed silent.

'Planes often hit turbulence when they reach the North Pennines,' said Trewick after a few moments. 'Maybe it worked a wire loose.'

'But is there also not a chance that you could have made a mistake when you did your final checks?' asked Gallagher.

'My husband did nothing wrong!' exclaimed Margaret, unable to contain her emotion any longer. 'Has he not been tormented enough by what happened that night without you making such insinuations?'

'I appreciate...' began the sergeant.

'I have gone over the events of that afternoon a thousand times,' said Trewick. His eyes assumed a haunted expression. 'I have gone over every single thing I did and I did nothing wrong, I'm sure of it. Whatever made that plane crash, it was not my fault.'

He started coughing, his body wracked by spasms. The detectives waited for him to regain his strength. It took several minutes.

'Patricia Malahide...' began Gallagher when the coughing had stopped.

'Don't listen to anything that woman says!' exclaimed Margaret. She spat the words out. 'She'll blame anyone but her beloved Ray and she does not care whose reputation she blackens! You should have seen the way that people looked at James after she said those things about the company to the local paper.'

Trewick started coughing again and gripped the arm of the chair as his body was wracked by yet more spasms. His face was twisted in pain.

'Do you have to keep doing this?' asked Margaret. She looked beseechingly at them. She was close to tears again.

'No, we don't,' said Roberts. 'Time to let it go, Matty. This is cruel.'

Gallagher nodded and stood up.

'Thank you for your time, Mr Trewick,' he said. 'I'm sure we'll not be troubling you again.'

Outside the house, the sergeant breathed in the fresh air with relief then took out his mobile phone to call Harris.

* * *

'That's the last of them,' said George Fenchurch. He closed the box containing aircraft parts and walked across the warehouse to where Alistair Marshall was standing.

'Nothing?' asked the detective constable.

'Of course not,' snapped Fenchurch. 'You can ring your boss and tell him that we have just wasted a lot of time on his wild goose chase. If only he had had the decency to...'

Marshall wondered whether or not he should interrupt the flow of complaints but something about the expression on the investigator's face made him think twice. Instead, the detective thought of the long journey north that lay ahead of them and sighed heavily.

'I take it that you are going to drive me home?' said Fenchurch when he had finished his rant. 'It'll be better than being stuck in that smelly old Land Rover. The thing was a tip.'

Marshall thought of the burger boxes and plastics drinks bottles strewn across the back seat of his own car and nodded gloomily; the thought of seven hours in the car with George Fenchurch, including, doubtless, an extended lecture on the evils of litter, filled the constable with dread.

'I'll ring the governor first,' he said.

'Yes, you do that,' replied Fenchurch. 'And you be sure to tell him what I said.'

'I'm sure he's heard it before,' said Marshall.

Fenchurch scowled at him.

* * *

After taking calls from Gallagher and Marshall in quick succession, Jack Harris slipped the mobile back into his jacket pocket and shook his head at Curtis and Armannsson.

'Bad news?' said Curtis.

'Only what we expected,' said Harris.

'That seals it then,' said Curtis. 'We'll scale things down. Jenny, may I suggest that you and your team return to Manchester? Jack, the two of you can always meet up if needs be.'

'I'm sure we can,' said Harris.

The more Armannsson thought back on the conversation later, on what would turn out to be a long and silent journey back to Manchester with her team, the more she became convinced that there had been a twinkle in the inspector's eye when he made the comment. Hard as she tried to convince herself otherwise, the idea persisted, even though she was not sure if she liked the thought or not – having Jack Harris as your only friend in the world did not feel like a particularly comfortable place to be.

After watching as the fraud squad car headed up the hill towards the marketplace, Harris returned to his office where he was watching the dogs eat their tea from bowls in the corner of the room when his mobile rang again. Harris took the call.

'Matty lad,' he said. The inspector could hear the sound of a car in the background. 'You on your way back then?'

'Yup, but I've got some interesting news for you. I've just had a call from the CPS. They want to prosecute the kids over the Passenger Eleven film.'

'Really?' said Harris. 'I thought they were going to overlook it because of the National Crime Agency investigation?'

'Yeah, so did I but the lawyer I spoke to wants them picking up.'

'On what charge?'

'The lad who rang it in with making a malicious 999 call, and the others for wasting police time.'

'You'll get no argument but I really did think that they'd opt for a slap on the wrists.'

'The CPS wants to make an example of them. Apparently, there has been a spate of hoax calls in the North West and they are looking at launching a public awareness campaign.'

'About time.'

'Yeah, it's a joint thing with all the emergency services. There's going to be a TV advert next month. Brian Blessed sitting on a horse and shouting into a big phone or something. The lawyer reckons our case will show that the CPS means business.'

'That'll please the mountain rescue lads. Hoax calls send Bob Crowther scatty. Are you and Gillian going to head over to Newcastle to pick them up on your way back?'

'My mate at the NCA has asked if we can delay it until Monday so they can tie up some loose ends.'

'Fair enough. We'll let them stew over the weekend. It'll do them good to think about what they have done. You come back here and get some rest in before tonight's burglary operation. It promises to be a long night. And a cold one, as well. It's due to drop below freezing tonight.'

'You do know how to show a girl a good time,' said Gallagher.

* * *

The afternoon light had long since faded by the time the black saloon car left Manchester and headed north in the headlights of the tea-time rush hour traffic. Lying on the back seat, concealed beneath a blanket, were two baseball bats. The passenger reached forward to set the sat nav.

'What's the name of the place again?' he asked.

'Mile End,' said the driver. 'About twenty miles north of Levton Bridge.'

The passenger fiddled with the device.

'Fucking hell,' he said once he had set the co-ordinates, 'it's in the middle of nowhere!'

'Less chance of being spotted,' said the driver. He turned towards the passenger and grinned. 'Less chance of someone disturbing us when we're having our fun.'

Chapter eighteen

Nine thirty that evening found Jack Harris and Matty Gallagher sitting in the inspector's Land Rover, which was parked with its lights off on a farm track close to the main valley road, four miles north of Levton Bridge. Neither man had spoken for twenty minutes and, lulled by the warmth emanating from the vehicle's heater, Gallagher was battling to keep his eyes open as the exertions of the day caught up with him.

Making a determined effort to stay awake, the sergeant peered out of the window and sighed; a man who was more used to the noise and bright lights of London, he had always struggled with the cloying silence that enveloped the valley on winter nights. A chatty companion would have helped pass the time but, the shadowy figure in the driver's seat, Jack Harris, did not do chatty. Gallagher tried to elicit conversation anyway. Gallagher always tried.

'Where did you leave it with Jenny Armannsson then?' he asked. 'You still friends?'

'Why shouldn't we be?'

'All this malarkey about sabotaged planes was down to her, wasn't it?'

'I went along with it,' said Harris. 'We all did.'

'But did we?' Gallagher shifted in his seat as his back protested at the angle at which he had been sitting. 'We all had our doubts. And what evidence did she have? Some vague claims by an anonymous informant – hardly justifies stirring things up the way we have, does it?'

'Hindsight is a wonderful thing, Matty lad. I've lost count of the number of crimes it has solved. Besides, not everyone thinks we're wasting our time. Edward Gough's sister, for one. And Patricia Malahide.'

'You wouldn't exactly want to stand them up before a jury, would you, though?' said Gallagher. 'A criminal's sister and a gold-digging widow. Patricia Malahide has rung me three times today. What's Armannsson's take on it all?'

Realising that the sergeant was not going to give up on his attempt to spark a conversation, Harris thought about the question for a minute.

'She's worried about what people will think,' said the inspector. 'There's plenty at GMP who will be delighted that their hot-shot female DI has ballsed up. People like Danny Caulker will not let this go. According to Jenny, he's done nothing but try to undermine her.'

Gallagher gave his boss a sly look.

'And did you comfort her?' he asked.

Harris did not reply but the sergeant saw a slight smile playing on the inspector's lips.

'You have entirely the wrong idea about me,' he said.

'Have I now?' Gallagher stared out into the darkness. 'We're wasting our time here as well.'

'Curtis is keen on it.'

'I know, but no burglar worth his salt is going to try anything when the media have already reported that we're launching our initiative, is he?' said Gallagher. 'It got five minutes on the local telly news tonight, for God's sake. That pretty redhead reporter standing outside the factory and interviewing Curtis.'

'That'll have pleased him. He likes getting his mug on the telly does our beloved leader.'

'Yeah, but we might as well have put up a big neon sign, saying "come here and get yourselves nicked".'

'But it's good PR, Matty lad. It's sending a message to the villains. Levton Bridge Police are being proactive. We are countering fear of crime in the rural area.'

'You sound like Curtis in his interview,' grunted Gallagher. 'That's the kind of thing he was saying.'

'I know you're tired but there's no need to get abusive.'

Gallagher gave a low chuckle.

'Sorry,' he said.

Harris reached out for the radio.

'Gillian,' he said. 'Anything happening at your end? The sergeant's getting bored.'

There was a crackling sound, then they heard the detective inspector's voice.

'Your sparkling repartee not enough to keep him entertained?' said Roberts.

'It would seem not,' said Harris.

'You tried giving him one of the colouring books? He might like the one with the giraffes. You never know, it might keep him quiet for a few minutes.'

'Oh, ha ha,' said Gallagher.

* * *

The black car drove slowly towards the hamlet shortly after 9.30pm. Cutting the headlights, the driver brought the vehicle to a halt before the buildings began and he and his accomplice sat and surveyed the single row of cottages that made up High End. The driver spotted, some distance beyond the other homes, a bungalow with an outside light illuminating the drive.

'There,' he said. He pointed and glanced across at his passenger. 'That one.'

'You sure?'

'That's what he said. Bungalow with a garage.'

'I'm still worried about that operation the cops are running,' said the passenger.

'I've told you, Perry wants it doing tonight. Besides, there's no way they can be everywhere. It could even work in our favour. They'll think it's a routine break-in.' The driver cut the engine. 'Let's go on foot, though. Don't want to alert folks.'

His accomplice nodded, wound down his window and tossed his cigarette out, the butt glowing orange for a few seconds before fading. The men left the vehicle and stood for a few moments as they listened to the night. More used to the city and its restless noises, they found themselves unnerved by the darkness and a silence punctuated only by the occasional plaintive bleat of sheep high up on the hills. The driver opened the rear door and took out the baseball bats, one of which he handed to his accomplice. The men walked slowly past the cottages, watching nervously for signs of movement in the windows, until to their relief they reached the bungalow undetected.

The driver looked at the light shining through the curtains in one of the downstairs rooms.

'Looks like they're in,' he said in a low voice. 'Excellent. Come on, let's get this over with.'

'Yeah, the sooner we get out of this place the better.' The accomplice shivered. 'It's far too fucking quiet. Give me Manchester any day.'

'Agreed.' The driver held up his bat. 'And remember what the man said, make it look good.'

His accomplice gave a crooked grin, revealing uneven teeth.

'Be my pleasure,' he said.

* * *

The silence had lengthened in the Land Rover.

'I know that silence,' said Gallagher. 'It means that you're thinking. What are you thinking?'

117

'I am thinking,' said Harris, reaching into the footwell for his flask of coffee, 'that I get this nagging feeling whenever everyone says the same thing. It either means that they are all good community-minded citizens who are telling the truth or that they've all got the same script.'

'Did you say anything to Curtis?'

'What could I say? He already thinks that I have been trying to wheedle my way out of tonight. And yet I can't help feeling that we're missing something, Matty lad. If I'm honest, I don't really understand all this fraud squad and air investigation stuff and that makes me feel uneasy. I like to understand what I'm investigating.'

'Amen to that,' said the sergeant. 'So, what do you think we're missing then?'

'If I knew that, I wouldn't be sitting here,' said Harris. He poured himself a drink. 'I'd be Chief Constable.'

'God help us if that ever happens,' said Gallagher.

'And you'd be helping pensioners across the road outside the day care centre.'

'See,' said Gallagher, 'you are developing a sense of humour.'

'Who said it was a joke?'

'Ah, well,' said the sergeant. 'Baby steps, eh?'

And he returned to staring out into the night.

* * *

The two men walked up the drive to the cottage, baseball bats held down by their sides. The driver reached the front door first, glanced round to check that no one had observed their arrival and gave a light knock. It took a good minute for the hall light to come on.

'Who is it?' said a woman's voice. She sounded frail and nervous.

The driver gave a slight smile; just as he liked them.

'Mrs Fenchurch?' he said in a low voice.

'Yes.'

'We're from the police.'

'What do you want?'

'It's nothing to worry about, ma'am,' said the driver. 'We're running an anti-burglary initiative in the area and just wanted to check that everything is OK. We're calling at some of the area's more remote houses. We're checking everyone in the village.'

Behind the door, Elizabeth Fenchurch nodded her appreciation. She had seen the item on that evening's local television news and had been reassured by the thought that the police were out in force in the area. A woman in increasingly poor health, she always felt vulnerable when her husband was not at home, particularly at night. George had been away for several days and had that evening telephoned to say that he and the detective constable had been delayed by hold-ups on the motorway, would not be back until after eleven and that she was not to wait up. The presence of the police in the hamlet was welcome.

Elizabeth opened the door to be confronted by two masked men.

'Where's the jewellery?' said one of them. He pushed her roughly back into the cottage, slammed the door and brandished the bat in her face. 'Where's the fucking jewellery?'

'But it's not worth anything,' she gasped.

The man lashed out with the bat, catching her a glancing blow on the right cheek. Elizabeth cried out and slumped to the ground, blood spurting from a deep cut. The man leaned down, bringing his face up to hers, so close that she could smell the nicotine on his breath.

'I said,' he rasped, 'where's the fucking jewellery?'

'I told you, it's not...'

The man raised his bat again.

Chapter nineteen

Alistair Marshall brought the car to a halt outside the bungalow in High End shortly after eleven and looked across at his passenger.

'Journey's end,' he said.

The detective constable knew that his tone of voice betrayed the relief he felt. Not that he cared what George Fenchurch thought any more. The long hours in the warehouse had tested the constable's civility to its limit and the homeward journey had proved an ordeal. What little conversation there had been between the two men had consisted of Fenchurch's gripes about the police but, to the constable's relief, it had faded away as they crawled through the third set of major roadworks somewhere near Manchester. They had not spoken for the remainder of the journey, other than the occasional grunted comment.

'Thank you for the lift,' said Fenchurch as he unbuckled his seatbelt. But he did not sound grateful.

He looked expectantly across at the detective, who sighed, got out of the vehicle and removed the investigator's bag from the boot. By the time the detective had recovered it, Fenchurch was already half way up the drive.

'I'm not a fucking taxi driver,' murmured Marshall, using a knee to push his way through the gate as he struggled with the bag.

As he did so, the detective noticed that Fenchurch had stiffened and had stopped walking. Dropping the bag and hurrying up behind him, the constable noticed that the front door of the bungalow was ajar.

'Does your wife normally do that?' he asked.

'Of course, she doesn't,' snapped Fenchurch. He sounded worried. 'I tell her to keep it locked when I'm away. We're very security conscious.'

'Let me go first,' said Marshall.

'But…'

'Let me go first,' repeated the constable. His voice brooked no dissent.

Marshall brushed past Fenchurch and, heart pounding and palms sweating, the constable cautiously pushed open the door and stepped over the threshold. All was quiet in the bungalow, but the detective instinctively sensed that something was wrong. Badly wrong.

'Mrs Fenchurch!' he shouted. He tried to sound more confident than he felt. 'It's the police!'

George Fenchurch followed him into the hallway.

'Elizabeth!' he called. 'Where are you?'

Marshall entered the living room. With mounting alarm, he surveyed the upturned furniture and the drawers and papers that had been strewn across the floor. The constable noticed smears of blood on one of the armchairs and closed his eyes for a moment. When he opened them again, Fenchurch was staring at the scene with an appalled look on his face.

'Oh, God, no,' he breathed.

'Mrs Fenchurch!' shouted Marshall as he headed back into the hallway. 'Are you OK?'

He heard a low moan from the direction of the kitchen and both men rushed into the room to see that more drawers had been ripped out and their contents hurled across the floor. Elizabeth Fenchurch was lying by the back door with blood pouring from the gaping wound on her cheek, one eye swollen and half-closed and a large bruise forming on her forehead. Her skin was pale and rimed with sweat and her breathing was shallow and erratic.

Fenchurch gave a cry and crouched down to cradle her head. For a few moments, it seemed that she did not realise it was her husband, then recognition flickered across her face and she gripped his hand.

'They kept asking for the jewellery,' she said weakly. Her voice was so low that it was scarcely audible. 'I told them it wasn't worth anything but they wouldn't listen.'

Elizabeth's voice tailed off, her grip slackened and her eyes fluttered and closed. Alistair Marshall closed his own eyes; the ramifications were already playing out in his mind. He took the mobile phone out of his jacket pocket and summoned an ambulance. Call made, he rang Harris.

The ringing of the inspector's phone brought Gallagher back to wakefulness as he was drifting into sleep in the passenger seat.

'Harris,' said the inspector, taking the call.

'It's Alistair,' said the constable. 'I think that you'd better get up to High End, sir. Someone's broken into George Fenchurch's home and attacked his wife.'

Harris put the phone on speaker so that Gallagher, now wide awake, could hear.

'When was this?' asked the inspector.

He looked at Gallagher and mouthed the words 'Elizabeth Fenchurch'. The sergeant closed his eyes.

'We've just found her,' said Marshall. 'I think it probably happened in the past couple of hours.'

'How is she?' asked Harris.

'She's been pretty badly beaten up. I'm just hoping that the ambulance can get here in time.' Marshall hesitated. 'I'm sorry, sir, but I think this might turn into a murder.'

'On our way,' said Harris. He ended the call, turned the key in the ignition and looked across at Gallagher. 'I told you that something was missing.'

'At least we understand murders,' said the sergeant.

Chapter twenty

The ambulance crew were bringing the unconscious Elizabeth Fenchurch out of the bungalow on a stretcher when Harris and Gallagher pushed their way through the front gate. Walking beside his wife, George heard the click of the latch, looked in their direction and turned hate-filled eyes on the inspector.

'This is your fault,' rasped Fenchurch. He jabbed an accusing finger at the detective. 'If you had not sent me on that wild goose chase, I would have been here to protect her!'

'No one could have foreseen this,' said Harris.

'You foresaw enough to launch an anti-burglary operation,' snapped Fenchurch. He watched the ambulance crew load Elizabeth into their vehicle. 'And plaster it all over the television. You must have known that something like this could happen.'

'We had no specific information, George.'

Fenchurch gestured towards the ambulance; he appeared to be fighting back tears.

'Is this specific enough for you?' he said, his voice trembling with emotion.

Before Harris could reply, Alistair Marshall emerged from the house and walked over to them.

'What do we know?' asked Harris.

'According to Mrs Fenchurch, they kept asking her where the jewellery was,' said the constable. 'She said they seemed to think that she had some expensive items.'

Harris looked at George.

'Could you have been targeted?' he asked. 'Perhaps someone saw your wife wearing an expensive piece of jewellery at an event and decided...?'

'Don't talk rot, man!' exclaimed Fenchurch, anger replacing grief. 'Of course, they didn't!'

'It's possible.'

'Do we look like the kind of people who'd have that kind of thing? And if you are suggesting that my wife is responsible for what has just...'

'Of course I'm not,' said Harris quickly; he'd read the Chief Constable's recent memo exhorting his officers to take a more sensitive approach to victims following a series of complaints across the force area. And he knew that George Fenchurch would think nothing of reporting him. Indeed, he would take great delight in doing so. 'I just need to be sure that...'

'Mr Fenchurch!' shouted one of the ambulancemen as his colleague closed the vehicle's door. 'We're going.'

'If Elizabeth dies...' said Fenchurch. He jabbed a finger in the inspector's direction again. Fenchurch did not finish the sentence but instead glared at Harris and stalked down the drive.

'How is she?' Harris asked Marshall when Fenchurch was out of earshot.

'The paramedics reckon it's touch and go. Whoever did this, gave her a real good doing over. She's got fractured ribs, a broken arm and maybe a fractured skull.'

'Nasty,' said Gallagher.

'Yeah, and they didn't need to do it,' said Marshall with a shake of the head. 'Even if she did resist them, she's not very strong. According to George, she's not been well for some time. Some kind of kidney problem that's been getting worse. There's no way that she would have been able to stop them.'

'Then why use such violence?' asked Gallagher.

'Why indeed?' said Harris.

'What are you thinking?'

'I am thinking that it might be someone sending a message.'

'What kind of message?' asked Gallagher. 'And to whom? Fenchurch?'

'Not sure yet. But I told you we were missing something.' Harris watched George Fenchurch climb into the back of the ambulance. 'Go with them, will you, Alistair? See if she says anything else. Give Matty the keys to your car. We'll drop it back in Levton Bridge.'

Marshall tossed the keys to the sergeant and jogged down to the ambulance. A few seconds after he had clambered in, the vehicle pulled away and headed off in the night, its blue light illuminating the darkness.

'Doesn't look good,' said Gallagher, watching it go.

'No, indeed.' Harris glanced back at the small knot of people now gathered outside the nearby cottages, watching proceedings in solemn silence. 'Go and see if anyone saw anything, will you, Matty lad? They could not have arrived without someone noticing them. Somebody must have seen something.'

'Will do.'

After Gallagher had gone, Harris walked into the bungalow and made his way into the living room. Deep in thought, he stood alone in a heavy silence punctuated only by the ticking of a carriage clock. *Then why use such violence?* Harris walked over to the mantelpiece, picked up the clock and read the inscription on the back – 'Good luck with the new job, hope you never have to investigate us! From all at Northern Airlines'. Harris put the clock back and turned to survey the items strewn across the floor. Something caught his eye and he crouched down to pick up a smashed picture frame. The inspector turned it over and stared at the image of a younger George Fenchurch, dressed in a captain's uniform and standing with his crew in front of a Northern Airlines jet aeroplane. Ranged behind him were a number of mechanics.

'I wonder,' murmured Harris.

His reverie was disturbed by the arrival of Gillian Roberts and Alison Butterfield.

'Jesus,' said Roberts, looking at the mess. 'They made a good job of it, didn't they?'

'Too good,' said Harris.

'Meaning?'

'Something's not right about this, Gillian. I'm getting a feeling.'

Roberts gestured to the drawers strewn across the floor.

'Do we assume that they were looking for something specific?' she asked.

'According to Alistair, they'd got it into their heads that she had some expensive jewellery.'

'And had she?' asked Roberts.

'George Fenchurch says not.'

'Perhaps he didn't know,' said Roberts. 'Lots of men have no idea what's in their wife's jewellery box. Mine certainly doesn't. I could have the Koh-i-Noor diamond in there, for all he knows.'

'Maybe.' Harris looked at Butterfield. 'Matty's interviewing the villagers, give him a hand, will you?'

When the constable had left the room, Harris looked at Roberts.

'Tell me,' he said, 'why would someone get it into their head that Elizabeth Fenchurch owns high-end jewellery?'

'You know what our local scroats are like. Chinese whispers. Someone thinks they've heard something, passes it on and before you know it the thing has ballooned out of all proportion. We can ask around our local low-lifes, see if the word was out that there was something worth nicking.'

'Would we not have heard already, though?'

'Maybe the robbers were from away,' said Roberts. 'I talked to Traffic about tonight's operation – they tracked thirty-one vehicles turning off the M6 onto roads that could potentially take them into the valley and quite a few were from outside the area.'

'Anything interesting?'

'None of them raised an alarm on ANPR but it wouldn't exactly be the first time that villains came in to rob houses here, would it?'

'I guess not.'

'But you don't sound convinced.'

'I'm not, Gillian.' Harris wafted a hand at the chaos. 'There's far too much violence involved. And doesn't it seem one hell of a coincidence that the only house that gets hit belongs to the guy who's been re-investigating the plane crash?'

'You've been listening to too many conspiracy theories,' said the detective inspector. 'You'll be telling me that Lord Lucan is responsible for this next. Besides, there could have been other houses broken into tonight. We might just not have heard yet. Folks getting back from a night out, that sort of thing.'

'And if there haven't been any?'

Roberts did not reply.

'Exactly,' said Harris. 'However, I take the point. We need to shake some trees and see what falls out.'

'I'll get the troops onto it.'

'Thanks. You and me can pop in on Crime Central when we get back to town.'

'Always a pleasure,' said Roberts.

Gallagher walked into the room and surveyed the chaotic scene.

'Boy, they meant business, didn't they?' he said.

'Indeed,' replied Harris. 'You get anything from the villagers?'

'There *was* a car. A black one. One of the residents saw it leaving the village but thought nothing of it. She just assumed that it was someone who had been visiting one of the houses. She thought it might have had two people in it. No description. Too dark.'

'She get a reg?'

'Only partial.' Gallagher held up his notebook and showed the page to Harris.

'That looks like a Manchester number,' said the inspector. He glanced at Roberts. 'And where were John Graydon and his little pals based?'

'My money's still on a robbery gone bad,' said Roberts.

Harris realised that he was still holding the picture of George Fenchurch and the air crew and placed it back on the dresser. Gallagher looked at it.

'I know that face,' he said. The sergeant pointed to one of the mechanics. 'Much younger, but that looks like James Trewick.'

Roberts walked over to join him in his perusal of the picture and nodded.

'That's him, alright,' she said.

'Really?' Harris looked at the picture with renewed interest. 'Did we know that he worked with Fenchurch?'

'I don't think we did,' said Gallagher. 'Trewick certainly did not mention it when we saw him.'

'Even if they did work together, I'm not sure that it means anything,' said Roberts. 'I imagine it's a pretty small world. They probably all know each other. I mean, Fenchurch knew Ray Malahide as well, didn't he? Worked with him, I believe.'

Before Harris could reply, his smartphone rang. The inspector took the call and listened grim-faced for a few moments before ending the call and slipping the phone back into his coat pocket.

'Well, whoever's behind it,' he said, 'we need to come up with some answers and we need to do it quickly. That was Alistair. Elizabeth Fenchurch just died in the ambulance.'

Chapter twenty-one

'You might as well know that my patience is running thin,' said Jack Harris sternly. He let his gaze roam round the room, then scowled. An old trick. 'Very thin indeed.'

It was just past 11.30pm and the inspector and Gillian Roberts were standing in the lounge of The George, the shabbiest of the pubs off Levton Bridge Market Place. The detectives had arrived a couple of minutes previously and Harris had immediately ordered most of the drinkers to leave, ignoring their loud protestations about half-finished pints and ushering the last of them through the door into the night-time drizzle with a hefty shove on the back. A uniformed officer had been posted at the front door of the pub to ensure that no one tried to get back in and he now stood, flapping his arms to keep warm, as the drinkers gradually melted away into the darkness, grumbling their dissatisfaction at what had happened.

The only people who had been prevented from leaving The George were two scruffy young men sitting nervously at a corner table and two, older shifty-looking men perched on stools at the bar. All four of them surveyed the inspector uneasily. They knew from hard experience that an encounter with Jack Harris was bad enough, but that one in which he was running out of patience could be truly nightmarish. Jack Harris, for his part, was enjoying himself immensely as he noted their discomfort. After a week in which he had wrestled with shadowy criminals whose existence was detectable only through rows of figures on balance sheets that meant little to him, the inspector was back in his comfort zone, dealing with crooks that he could see and understand.

'So, gentlemen,' said Harris, looking at the men, 'I'm sure that you will be only too keen to offer us your assistance on what is a very serious matter.'

Roberts stood by the window and watched the men's nervous expressions with a faint smile on her face. She had witnessed the inspector's performance so many times before that she knew the routine. Roberts also knew that the men in the room, all of them notorious local thieves, would be panicking as they desperately tried to work out why Harris had homed in on them. It had always amused the detective inspector that the town's criminals thought that their plotting in The George was happening well away from prying police eyes when, in fact, Harris only let it happen because he preferred to have them where he knew he could find them in situations like this.

'After all,' said Harris with a disarming smile, 'we don't want any unpleasantness, do we now?'

Without realising he had done it, one of the younger men held a hand to his face, feeling again the sharp sting of the slap that Harris had delivered when he had answered back during a fractious encounter with the detective the previous year. Roberts noticed the gesture and frowned; she had never quite come to terms with the way the inspector walked the line in an area where he let everyone know that he was the law. However, the thought of Elizabeth Fenchurch lying dead in the ambulance with her distraught husband by her side persuaded her that sometimes the ends justified the means.

'You wish to offer us some pearls of wisdom?' said Harris, noticing the young man's action.

'I ain't done nothing wrong. What's this about anyway?'

'A woman died up at High End tonight,' said Harris. 'Lady by the name of Elizabeth Fenchurch. Beaten to death by someone who broke in to steal jewellery. The kind of stroke you lot would pull, given half a chance.'

The men looked worried. Stealing was one thing but murder raised the stakes to a new level. During a murder inquiry, things to which the police turned a blind eye in normal circumstances suddenly assumed great importance. Life could become very awkward indeed and they all knew it.

'We don't know nothing,' said the young man quickly. 'And I've heard nowt about some bird having jewellery neither.'

He looked to the others for confirmation and they all nodded their agreement.

'He's right,' said one of the older men. 'No one's been talking about it. We'd have heard if they were. And there's no way that we'd kill anyone. You know that, Mister Harris.'

'Maybe I do,' said the inspector. He fixed them with another hard look. 'Or maybe you're only telling me half the story, as usual. Maybe you brought in a bit of muscle in case her husband tried to stop you?'

'Couldn't have been us,' said the other young man. He grinned, revealing yellowing and crooked teeth. 'There ain't no late bus back from High End.'

None of the others laughed and Gillian Roberts shook her head at the stupidity of youth. She held her breath as Harris walked slowly across to tower over him. The young man's smile faded and he went pale.

'You think this is funny, do you, son?' said Harris. His voice was quiet and laden with menace. 'The murder of a sick, elderly woman something to make a joke about, is it?

My sergeant keeps saying that I am developing a sense of humour but, to be honest, I am struggling to see the joke.'

'No, no,' said the man quickly. He shrank into his seat as Harris leaned over until their faces were just inches apart. 'No, of course I don't think it's funny.'

Roberts wondered if she would have to intervene but, to her relief, Harris grunted and walked back to the middle of the room.

'So, if it wasn't any of you,' said the inspector, 'maybe it's down to an outside crew?'

'How would we know about that?' said one of the older men.

'Come off it!' exclaimed Harris. 'We all know that you fence your high-end gear in Liverpool. And last time I looked at your list of known associates, they included half the crooks in the North West! Stop playing games – I really am not in the mood.'

'OK, so maybe I did deal with them once or twice in the past,' said the man guardedly. He sensed that he had to say something to pacify Harris. 'But I don't know nothing about no murder, Mister Harris. Honest.'

The other men nodded their heads again and Harris pondered the comment.

'OK,' he said. The inspector turned to go. 'But if I hear anything different, so help me…'

Leaving the threat hanging in the air, the detectives left the pub, relieved the uniformed officer of his guard duties at the door and walked across the marketplace, the rain on the cobbles glistening in the glow of the street lights.

'What do you think?' asked Harris as they reached the darkened shops on the far side of the square.

'I think they're telling the truth,' said Roberts. 'Violence like that is just not their style.'

'But what if they were disturbed, like you said? Elizabeth Fenchurch walks in on them and they panic? Lose their cool? Lash out? Not exactly unknown, is it?'

'Still can't see it,' said Roberts. The officers left the marketplace and started walking down the hill towards the police station. 'My money's on outsiders.'

'Not on a link to the air crash?'

'You know my views on that. We'd be chasing shadows.'

'Maybe, but if no one was talking about Elizabeth Fenchurch having jewellery, why was the house targeted?'

'Now there's a question I can't answer,' said Roberts.

The detectives walked in silence for the remainder of the way down to the station, relieved to see that there were no journalists standing outside; news of the murder had not been released to the media and word had clearly not leaked out yet. Once inside the building, they climbed the stairs to the inspector's office to pick up the dogs, then walked along the darkened corridor to the CID room where they found a number of officers hard at work. Matty Gallagher was just putting the phone down as they walked in.

'Who was that?' asked Harris.

'Leckie ringing back,' said the sergeant. 'You asked him to check their records for the Manchester car, I think?'

'And?'

'Reported stolen this afternoon. Belongs to a GP. Nicked when he was on a house call. According to Leckie, the doctor is straight and there's no link with what happened up here.'

'There's a surprise,' said Harris. Wearily, he sat down at one of the desks by the window and stared out into the darkness.

'How'd it go with the delightful denizens of Crime Central?' asked the sergeant.

'They don't know anything.' Harris looked at Roberts. 'It's beginning to look like we are dealing with something bigger than our local tea leaves. The DI reckons it's guys coming in from the outside. Pros.'

'Pros don't kill old women,' said Gallagher.

'Some do,' said Roberts. 'Especially if they don't realise how frail their victim is. Leckie have anything else?'

'They've got plenty who have done jobs up this way but no one linked with Elizabeth Fenchurch.' Gallagher glanced round at the other detectives. 'We've all been checking with our informants but none of them knew anything about her having any jewellery.'

'Yeah, we drew a blank in The George as well.' Harris thought of the ransacked rooms in the bungalow. 'Well, they were looking for something.'

He glanced up at the wall clock. Eleven fifty.

'Alistair still down at the hospital?' he asked.

'He just rang in,' said Gallagher. 'Fenchurch is adamant that he doesn't want to talk to anyone until the morning. Says that if he sees you tonight, he'll end up saying something he'll regret.'

'I can guess what that means,' said Harris bleakly. 'He's probably filling the complaint form in as we speak.'

'He's wrong, you know,' said Roberts. 'There's no way that his wife's death is your fault.'

Harris looked back into the room; every officer was nodding their agreement at the sergeant's comment.

'Thank you,' said Harris. He stood up. 'Much appreciated. I'm going to see him anyway. This is a murder inquiry and I'm not letting George Fenchurch call the shots. Gillian, meet me round the front in five minutes, will you? I have a little job to do before we go.'

* * *

A couple of minutes later, Harris was sitting at the desk in his office. He selected a name from the contacts file on his smartphone, stared at it pensively for a few moments then pressed the button. The call was picked up immediately.

'Jenny?' said Harris. 'It's Jack Harris. Sorry to ring you so late. Hope you're not in bed.'

'You should be so lucky,' said Armannsson. He could hear that she was smiling. 'But it's no problem. Leckie said that you'd probably get in touch. I heard what happened to George Fenchurch's wife. You think it's connected to our investigation?'

'I'm the only one that thinks that it might be. I wondered if you would do me a favour?'

'Sure. What do you want me to do?'

'The first thing I want you to do is promise to keep this between you and me for the moment,' said the inspector. He thought of the picture in the Fenchurch's living room. 'If this gets out and I'm wrong, there'll be hell to pay. What my commander likes to call a PR disaster.'

* * *

Five minutes later, Harris had ended the call and was bounding down the stairs, dogs behind him, on his way to meet Roberts when a voice called him back. The inspector looked up to see a grim-faced Philip Curtis at the top of the stairs. The commander walked down to meet him.

'You making any progress?' he asked.

'Not yet but it's early days.'

'Well, we need to clear this up quickly, Jack. More than thirty officers out on an anti-burglary operation and whoever did this got past all of you. The community has been demanding that we do something about burglaries for months and now this happens. Handled wrongly, this could be a PR disaster.'

'I'll bear that in mind, sir.'

Followed by the dogs, Harris walked down to the bottom of the stairs and pushed his way through the security door that led into the reception area.

* * *

The mobile phone rang as Perry St Martin sat in his spacious lounge, sipping on his third large whisky and continually glancing up at the wall clock. Ever careful, he checked the identity of the caller before hitting the receive button.

'You get it?' he asked eagerly.

He listened in grim silence for a few moments.

'I told you to make it look good,' hissed St Martin. 'Not fucking kill her! Are you sure she's dead?'

'That's what it said on the police radio,' said the driver. 'Look, I'm sorry, but we didn't mean for her to die. She was alive when we left her.'

'Well, she's fucking well dead now, isn't she?'

'I've said I'm sorry,' said the driver.

'Sorry won't cut it, you fucking moron!' snarled St Martin. 'Do you think sorry will be enough for Jack Harris? The fucking place will be swarming with cops. Did anyone see you?'

'I don't think so. We were very careful.'

'You'd better be right,' said St Martin. 'And you'd better be about to tell me that you found it.'

There was silence at the other end.

'You did get it, didn't you?' rasped the man.

'It wasn't there.'

'What do you mean it wasn't fucking well there?' said St Martin. He felt a knot twist in the pit of his stomach. 'It has to be there. He said he'd got it.'

'We looked everywhere,' said the driver. 'Did what you said, tried to make it look like we were after her jewellery, but I tell you it wasn't there. It must be somewhere else.'

'Well worked out, Einstein,' snapped St Martin. 'And Fenchurch wasn't there?'

'No. And there's no way we were waiting for him, not with her like that. What do you want us to do? We're wanted for murder now.'

'Where are you?'

'Back in Manchester.'

'Well, I want you to lay low,' said St Martin. 'Keep as far away from Jack Harris as possible. And don't contact me again.'

'But…'

St Martin ended the call, swore and blocked the number. Furiously, he hurled his glass across the room where it shattered on impact with the wall. Things were unravelling and Perry St Martin needed to think and think fast. He dialled another number on his phone.

'We've got a problem,' he said when the call was answered. 'I have this awful feeling that Jack Harris is coming for us.'

'But you said you were going to sort it.'

'I know what I said but something went wrong. Fenchurch's wife is dead.'

'Jesus! What are we going to do now?'

'Honest answer?' said St Martin. 'I don't know because, if I know one thing about Jack Harris, it's that if he comes after you, he doesn't stop until he's got you.'

Chapter twenty-two

'I told your officer that I didn't want to talk to you,' said George Fenchurch. His voice was trembling and he seemed close to tears. 'Why won't you just let me go home, Chief Inspector? I just want to go home.'

'I appreciate that, and I understand how upset you must be. I am truly sorry for your loss.'

It was well after midnight and Fenchurch was sitting with the inspector and Gillian Roberts in a side room on the third floor of Roxham General Hospital. He presented a very different figure from previous encounters: gone was the confident bearing, the sense of defiance, the arrogance, to be replaced by hunched shoulders and hooded eyes. George Fenchurch was a man who had been crushed by the evening's events.

'However,' continued Harris, 'this is a murder inquiry now and we do need to ask you some questions, I am afraid.'

'I just want to go home,' said Fenchurch again; his voice was barely audible this time. 'I don't want to talk to any of you. I want to be on my own.'

'I am afraid that will not be possible,' said Harris as sympathetically as he could manage. Which wasn't much.

'There is a forensics team at your home at the moment and they'll be there for several hours. I really think it would better if you found somewhere else to stay tonight.'

'What if I refuse?' A flash of the old defiance forced its way through the grief. 'What if I say that I want to go home? Demand that you take me back?'

'I can't let you go home, George. Not tonight.'

Fenchurch gave the inspector a baleful look. The anger burst through the grief.

'This is your fault,' he said vehemently. 'I could have protected her if you hadn't sent me to Hertfordshire.'

'I really do not think that's fair, Mr Fenchurch,' said Roberts as she noticed Harris struggling to keep his irritation under control. 'And the inspector's right, you really should not be on your own tonight. Believe me, lovey, it's for the best.'

She reached across to gently touch Fenchurch's hand in what she hoped was a gesture of reassurance. It usually worked. But not this time. Fenchurch withdrew his arm quickly and gave her a contemptuous look. Roberts gave the inspector a look of her own – 'do what you want', it said.

'Look,' said Harris, 'I know that you blame me for what happened to your wife but we had no idea that the people who did this were in the area. You have to believe me when I say that.'

'Yet you had all those officers looking out for them,' said Fenchurch. 'Try and explain that away.'

'We've already gone through this, George. We weren't looking specifically for them. It's just that when the dark nights arrive…'

Fenchurch snorted his derision. Harris sighed and glanced at Roberts, who shrugged.

'Before your wife died,' said Harris, 'she said that the men who attacked her were after her jewellery. Do you have any idea why they would think that she had something worth stealing?'

141

'Don't you think I would have told you if she did?' said Fenchurch angrily. 'She had nothing like that.'

'Nothing at all?' asked Roberts. 'Are you sure?'

Something about her gentle tone of voice finally got through to Fenchurch and he calmed down slightly. He shook his head.

'A couple of rings and a necklace that she inherited from her mother, that's all,' he said.

'Were they valuable, lovey?' asked Roberts.

'Not really. We had them valued three or four years back when we were changing house insurance companies. The jeweller said that the whole lot was not worth more than three hundred pounds. Bargain Hunt stuff, he said. Sentimental value only.' Fenchurch turned dark eyes on the detectives. 'Hardly worth killing for, is it?'

'No,' said Harris. 'No, it's not and our forensics team found them thrown onto the bedroom floor, so the intruders obviously came to the same conclusion about their worth. Is there any other reason why someone should break into your home?'

'Like what?' Fenchurch gave him a suspicious look. 'What are you trying to insinuate, Chief Inspector?'

'Nothing. I'm just trying to understand what happened tonight.'

'I'll tell you what happened,' said Fenchurch angrily. 'My wife was murdered and no one was there to protect her! That's what happened!'

'Yes, and we want to find out who did it,' said Harris. The inspector glanced at Roberts. 'This was the only incident tonight, wasn't it?'

'There's certainly been nothing else reported.'

'What of it?' asked Fenchurch. He seemed more guarded now. Choosing his words carefully. 'What relevance could that possibly have?'

'It just seems odd,' said Harris; the change in Fenchurch's demeanour had not gone unnoticed by either detective. 'We are wondering why your home was the only one targeted. You did not tell us that you worked with James Trewick.'

The change in tack surprised Fenchurch.

'What?' he said.

'There was a framed photograph showing the two of you. It was in your living room.'

'So?'

For the first time in the inspector's dealing with Fenchurch, the man looked worried. It was only a flicker of emotion on his face, there for but a second, but there all the same. Harris gave the slightest of sideways glances at Roberts, whose expression was impassive. But Harris knew what she was thinking.

'I'm sorry,' said Fenchurch, 'but I am not sure that I can see where this is leading.'

'I just thought it was interesting that the two of you knew each other from the days before you became an investigator.'

'Why on earth would it be interesting?' asked Fenchurch. He looked at the inspector with narrowed eyes. 'What kind of game are you playing?'

'Well, whoever killed your wife was looking for something,' said Harris. His mind was racing now, overflowing with options. He decided to push things further, see what reaction it brought from Fenchurch. 'I suspect that this was no random break-in. I think they were looking for something specific. And seeing the picture of James Trewick made me wonder if there could be…'

'Are you really trying to tell me that what happened tonight was linked to the air crash?' Fenchurch stared at him in amazement; he had regained his composure now. 'Is this the way you run your investigations? With snide insinuations?'

'We have to consider all possibilities.'

'You're mad! Absolutely crazy!' Fenchurch was shouting and he stood up and furiously jabbed a finger at the inspector. 'And I won't stay here to listen to such rubbish!'

'Calm down, George,' said Harris. He got to his feet as well.

'Calm down! When someone is saying such preposterous things!' Fenchurch glared at Harris and his next words were spoken in a voice that was calmer. Cold. Clipped. Laced with contempt. 'You just won't be told, will you? You've made a damned fool of yourself and you can't bring yourself to admit that crash was down to Ray Malahide. I will be making an official complaint about your conduct, you can be sure of that.'

'That's up to you but I would like to know a bit more about your original investigation into the crash. Did you, for example…?'

Fenchurch passed a hand across his eyes.

'I'm very tired,' he said. 'All this is very upsetting. Can we put an end to this nonsense?'

Harris nodded.

'Sure,' he said. Fenchurch's vehement response had given him much to ponder and he could see that Roberts felt the same. 'Look, I'm sorry if I upset you, George. It's just that I'm under pressure to catch the people who killed your wife. You're probably right about the crash. Like you say, it's time I faced up to the truth about it.'

'I'm glad you finally acknowledge it,' said Fenchurch grudgingly.

'The hospital has agreed to make up a room for you if you wish to stay here tonight,' said Roberts. 'One of the nurses is waiting outside.'

Fenchurch nodded.

'Thank you,' he said. Suddenly, he looked much older; the anger had subsided again and he seemed close to tears once more. 'Look, I'm sorry for having a go at you, Chief Inspector.'

'That's alright,' said Harris. 'It's entirely understandable in the circumstances. You're under a lot of stress.'

'I know but nevertheless it was out of order and I want to apologise. I know that I can be a difficult man but tonight has destroyed my world. You have to understand that. Elizabeth was everything to me.' Fenchurch reached out to touch the inspector's arm. 'Find out who killed her. Please.'

'We will,' said Harris.

As Roberts led Fenchurch out of the room, the investigator started to cry and slumped against the wall, his head held in his hands and his body wracked with sobs. The detectives left the room, giving him time to compose himself. Waiting in the corridor was Matty Gallagher's wife, who was one of the nurses.

'Just give him a minute,' said Harris.

'Yeah, will do,' said Julie. She peered into the room at the sobbing man. 'You finished?'

'For now.'

'Are you going to let my husband go home then?'

Harris gave a rueful smile. 'He should be wrapping up for the night as we speak. Look after George, yeah?'

'Sure.'

The detectives headed down the stairs and along the deserted hospital corridors before emerging into the crisp night air and the starlit sky. Half way across the car park, Roberts stopped and looked back at the hospital, trying to pick out the window of the room where they had interviewed Fenchurch. As she stood there, her empathetic human side did battle with her suspicious police officer side. As usual, the detective won out.

'Am I being unfair…?' she began.

'Probably.'

'You're too kind. What I was going to say was did that little act at the end strike you as put on? The tears and the grateful widower stuff?'

'I was thinking the exact same thing,' said Harris. 'And, oddly enough, it all started when I started asking him about the plane crash.'

'Maybe your instincts are right, after all,' said Roberts. 'Maybe there is a connection.'

'Maybe there is,' said Harris as they reached his Land Rover. 'But I am blessed if I know what it is. Not yet. Anyway, I can't prove anything so we'll let him stew on it overnight.'

His phone rang.

'Forensics,' he said and took the call as he unlocked the vehicle and clambered into the driver's seat. 'What you got for me, Beth? Tell me it's something good.'

'Sorry,' said the forensics officer. 'We've got nothing.'

'Nothing?'

'The house is as clean as a whistle, Jack. They probably wore gloves. We've come up with loads of prints but we're pretty sure that they belong to George Fenchurch and his wife. Oh, and we didn't find any more jewellery. We have looked everywhere but there is no way that Elizabeth Fenchurch had a secret stash. We found nothing.'

'Don't worry,' said Harris. 'I didn't think you would. I don't think it exists. You didn't find any pieces of aeroplane by any chance, did you?'

'Aeroplane?' asked Beth. 'No, nothing like that. Unless we missed a wing in the back garden.'

'I was thinking of something a bit smaller.'

'Sorry, nothing,' said Beth. 'Why do you ask?'

'Just a crazy thought. You finished there then?'

'We'll be about another hour. Your uniform lad's going to stand guard over the place when we leave.'

'Thanks, Beth,' said Harris. He ended the call and looked at Roberts, who was closing the passenger side door.

'Pieces of aeroplane?' she asked.

'Just a thought. See, whatever they were after, it wasn't jewellery.'

Roberts clicked her fingers. 'The altimeter!' she exclaimed. 'You think that they were looking for the altimeter!'

'I do.'

'Hang on, though.' Roberts frowned. 'That would mean that you think the crash was sabotage, after all. We have found nothing to suggest that. And why on earth would George Fenchurch have the altimeter anyway?'

'I suspect he doesn't. I think it's buried up on the hills somewhere but what would happen if someone thought that he did?' The inspector gave a knowing smile. 'Interesting, eh?'

'Jack Harris, I know that look,' said Roberts. 'You're planning something.'

Harris turned the ignition key and the engine rumbled into life.

'Always,' he said. 'But don't tell Curtis. Not yet anyway. There's no way I can risk bringing Fenchurch in for questioning until I'm sure. As Curtis keeps reminding me, the last thing we want is a PR disaster.'

Chapter twenty-three

Jack Harris cut an exasperated figure as he prowled round Mile End early the next morning, overseeing the door to door activities of his team and their uniformed colleagues. Every report only served to darken his mood as interview after interview failed to reveal any new recollections from the villagers. His demeanour was little improved by the call from Curtis shortly after ten, summoning him back to Levton Bridge Police Station to attend a press conference.

The call that he had been waiting for came just before noon and transformed his mood. The inspector was back in his office, staring out of the window as yet more rain fell from grey skies. He had just returned from the press conference in the main briefing room, during which he and Philip Curtis had tried their best to issue reassurances to the anxious community. The control room had been inundated with calls from worried members of the public ever since the force had released details of the murder of Elizabeth Fenchurch and, as they had left the briefing room, both men were acutely aware that they needed a breakthrough and they needed it quickly.

Now, Harris was sitting sipping at a mug of tea while constantly leaning forward to tap the screen on the smartphone on his desk as he checked that he had not missed a call. Time and time again, the words 'what if you're wrong?' forced their way to the front of his mind.

'Come on, Jenny,' he muttered. 'Where are you?'

When the phone finally did ring, the inspector snatched the device from the desk.

'Harris,' he said.

'Boy that was quick,' replied Jenny Armannsson.

'I've got a lot riding on this. I've just spent an hour telling the public that they are not going to be attacked in their beds by rampaging burglars. I'll look pretty stupid if I turn out to be wrong.'

'Well, they can rest easy, I suspect. It looks like you're right.'

'You've turned something up?'

'We have. Sorry it's taken so long. Bankers don't like working saturdays and it didn't help that he set up an account in a fake name. However, I think your instincts are right, Jack; there's a strong chance that George Fenchurch was specifically targeted. Pen at the ready?'

'Fire away,' said Harris as he fished around amidst the mass of papers strewn across his desk.

Ten minutes later, the inspector ended the call and sat staring down at the scribbled notes. A smile spread across his face.

'Got you,' he said quietly. The inspector frowned. 'I think.'

He dialled an internal number.

'Gillian,' he said. 'It's a go. Can you and Matty get over there and pick him up?'

'Are we sure about this?' asked the detective inspector. 'I mean, if we're not, we could be guilty of harassing a man who is in a very fragile condition. Think how bad that will look.'

'I know that, Gillian, but, at the very least, he's got some awkward questions to answer.'

'Like?'

'Like, how come the fraud squad have turned up a payment of £35,000 to him in the days after the crash?'

'On our way,' said Roberts.

* * *

Two hours later, the detective inspector and Matty Gallagher were standing outside James Trewick's house in Melrose. Roberts hesitated for a few moments, with her finger hovering over the doorbell. She glanced at Gallagher.

'You still not sure?' asked the sergeant.

'Not one hundred percent. I do hope that Hawk is right. There'll be hell to pay if he's not. I mean, the guy's in a desperate state.'

'It would be a PR disaster, alright,' said Gallagher. 'As our beloved commander likes to call them.'

'Here goes nothing then,' said Roberts.

She pressed the bell. It was a long time before the door was opened but when it finally swung open, it was clear that Margaret Trewick had been crying. She stared at them for a few moments through red-rimmed eyes.

'He's dead,' she said quietly. 'He died last night.'

'We are very sorry to hear that,' replied Roberts.

'So you can stop persecuting him,' exclaimed Margaret angrily. She tried to close the door. 'My husband's suffering is at an end.'

'Unfortunately, it's not that simple,' said Gallagher. He jammed his foot forward to prevent the door from closing. 'See, all those people who lost people in the crash, they're still suffering.'

'Yes, well, that's nothing to do with us.'

'Isn't it?'

Margaret tried to force the door closed again but the sergeant resisted. After struggling for a few moments, Margaret relented and stopped pushing.

'What exactly do you want?' she asked.

'We know about the £35,000,' said Gallagher.

Margaret stared at him in horror.

'You do?' she said and looked over to Roberts. 'You do?'

Roberts nodded.

'We do, lovey,' she said. 'Time to tell us what you know.'

The inspector's voice was soft. Reassuring. Genuine. She always felt sympathy for those who were hurt by the actions of others. Particularly loved ones who they believed they could trust. The thought made her issue herself an internal rebuke; they didn't yet know that they could trust Margaret Trewick. Too many people had been lying for that to be the case. The detective inspector noticed curtains twitching in the upstairs window of a house across the road.

'I think you'd better let us in, don't you?' she said. 'I am sure that you don't really want to have this conversation on the doorstep.'

Margaret had also noticed the curtain. She nodded and stood aside to let the officers enter the house.

'Am I under arrest?' she asked fearfully as she led them down the hallway. The fire of a few moments before had drained from her.

'It depends what you know and how long you have known it,' said Roberts.

'I only found out last night.' Margaret started to cry again. 'He told me just before he died.'

'Then I doubt very much that you will be prosecuted.'

Five minutes later, the officers were seated in the living room, acutely aware that the chair previously occupied by James Trewick was empty and that the oxygen cannister had gone. They could see the ring on the carpet where it had stood. Roberts took a sip of her tea and looked at Margaret, who was sitting clutching a handkerchief with which she occasionally dabbed her eyes.

'We are truly sorry for your loss,' said Roberts. 'Truly, we are.'

'What is it people say at times like this? That it was for the best? He had suffered terribly, had James.'

The detectives nodded as they thought back to their previous encounter and the emotions they had experienced as they watched Trewick battle for every breath. However, sitting in the trim little living room, any pity that they might have felt was rapidly banished by the thought of the bodies being carried off the hill following the air crash. There was work to do.

'But like you said,' continued Margaret, 'many other people have suffered because of what my husband did.'

'They have indeed,' said Gallagher. 'And you only found out last night?'

'Thirty-eight years married to him and it's like I didn't know the man.'

'Why do you think he decided to tell you?' asked the sergeant. 'I mean, after keeping the secret for all those years?'

'He said he didn't tell anyone because he wanted to protect us from any consequences. Whatever you might think, he was a good man was James. I think that he would have been prepared to go to prison but he was afraid what that might mean for me and the kids.'

'So, what changed last night?' asked Gallagher.

'He believed that it was only a matter of time before you found out the truth and I don't think he could face taking all that guilt to his grave. He said that the lying had to stop.'

'And you never suspected what he had done?' asked Gallagher. 'I mean, not once?'

'How could anyone suspect that of the man they love? I had always believed what James told me, that it was down to Ray Malahide. What did they call it? Pilot error.' She buried her head in her handkerchief. 'Oh, his poor wife. Living with people thinking that he caused all those deaths.'

'What exactly did James tell you?' asked Roberts.

Margaret hesitated.

'We'll find out anyway,' said Gallagher. 'We're putting the pieces together very quickly. It's only a matter of time. And whatever you say cannot harm him now. Or you and your family.'

Margaret nodded.

'I suppose you're right,' she said. She took a few moments to gather her thoughts. 'James said that a few days before the crash he was working in the Howletts hangar at Prestwick when a man he'd never seen before approached him. He said that he knew James had money problems.'

'What kind of money problems?' asked Roberts.

'The horses. We'd had some terrible rows about it. I thought he'd stopped gambling but it turns out that he hadn't. We were behind on our mortgage payments but I had no idea how bad it really was. James handled all our finances.' Margaret shook her head. 'All that happening and I knew nothing. I feel so stupid.'

'I wouldn't beat yourself up about it,' said Roberts. 'You'd be surprised how often it happens. We've all got secrets. What did this man want from James?'

'He said that he would pay off all our debts if James fixed it for the plane to crash.'

'And James agreed?'

'Not at first. He told me that the idea horrified him and he was going to tell the police. But the next day we had a letter from the building society. Looking back, I remember it. He looked worried for a moment but, when he saw that I was watching him, he said it was a marketing circular and scrunched it up and threw it on the fire.'

'Do you know what it really was?' asked Roberts.

'A letter threatening to repossess our home.'

'So, James changed his mind?' said Gallagher. 'Agreed to do it?'

'Yes. He said the idea made him feel sick but the kids were aged nine and ten and Lucy had been ill for months.

Bronchitis. James said he could not bear the thought of them being on the street so he agreed.'

'And how precisely did he do it?' asked Gallagher.

'He fixed the wiring on the altimeter to come loose once they were in the air. He said it was easy if you knew what you were doing. He said that planes often hit turbulence as they approached the Pennines and he thought that would shake the wire free. He knew that the Howletts didn't like pilots turning back because of the money it cost them.'

'He seems to have had it all worked out.'

'It was horrifying to hear the way he described it.' Margaret shook her head again. 'All those poor people. All those poor families.'

'And all the money he was paid went to pay off his debts, you say?' asked Roberts.

'Not all of it. We had some left over. We were never well off so it was welcome.'

'Didn't you think it odd when you suddenly had a bit of cash?' asked Gallagher.

'He said it was a bonus because the company had won a big contract. I did not ask too many questions. It was the answer to our prayers. James lost his job when Howletts went bust a few weeks later and it took him a long time to get back into work.' She gave a mirthless laugh. 'We even had our first holiday in years that summer. Can you believe it, two weeks of us and the kids on the funfair rides in Skegness paid for by the blood of those people?'

She fell silent and the room was quiet for a few moments.

'Hang on,' said Roberts as a thought struck her. 'You said that James had never seen the man who approached him before?'

'That's right, yes.'

'But we assumed it was George Fenchurch?' The inspector recalled the photograph she had seen at the investigator's house the previous night. 'They'd worked together before. They knew each other, surely?'

'They did, yes, but George Fenchurch didn't organise the crash. No, the man who approached James was called Perry St Martin. The man who had booked the flight for John Graydon.'

Gallagher glanced at Roberts; both detectives were bemused.

'But we have found records of large cash transactions going into Fenchurch's accounts at about the same time,' said the sergeant. 'We assumed it was because he had been paid to organise the crash.'

'The money was not for that. George Fenchurch may be many things but he is not a killer.' Her face twisted with revulsion. 'No, George Fenchurch is a parasite of the worst kind. Some might say that it is just as bad.'

* * *

Jack Harris strode into the Roxham General Hospital ward and up to the desk where Julie Gallagher was sitting updating her notes.

'Jack,' she said. 'What brings you here?'

'I am looking for George Fenchurch. Any idea where he is?'

'No, he left early. Told one of the nurses that he was going home. You could try him there.'

'He didn't make it. I thought he'd go straight home but he's disappeared. How did he seem?'

'I didn't see him, I am afraid. Is he in trouble?'

'You could say that.'

It was a grim-faced Harris who left the ward. Once out on the landing, he took his phone out of his pocket, looked round to make sure that no one could overhear his conversation, and made a call to the CID squad room.

'Alistair, it's Harris,' he said. 'I want an APB issued for George Fenchurch. Ports, airports, the lot. Yes, I'm sure.

Widower he may be but I remain to be convinced that he's grieving.'

* * *

Forty minutes later, Harris had made the journey back from Roxham and parked his Land Rover outside Levton Bridge Police Station. After letting the dogs out of the vehicle, he bounded up the front steps.

'Ah, just the man,' said the desk sergeant as the detective walked into the reception area. He gestured to a stern-faced grey-haired man and, standing next to him, a sickly-looking Davie Tinkler. 'They want a word.'

'Now's not a good time,' said Harris.

'I want to know what's happening,' said Bill Tinkler. He stood in the inspector's path as the detective headed for the door leading into the corridor. 'Is my son going to be prosecuted? I can't get any sense out of the National Crime Agency.'

'I'm a bit busy at the...'

'I really want to know.'

Harris was about to push past him but noticed the anxious look on Bill Tinkler's face and nodded.

'Of course,' he said. He gestured towards the interview room. 'I'm sorry. Come in here.'

Once they were seated, Harris looked across the desk at Bill.

'I can't speak for the National Crime Agency,' he said. 'We're not involved in that investigation and I'm not quite sure what's going to happen, but Davie is definitely going to be prosecuted for the hoax, yes.'

'But it was just kids mucking about!' protested Bill.

'Maybe so but the Crown Prosecution Service are cracking down on hoax calls. Look, I am not going to sugar coat this, Bill. They are going to throw the book at them for what they did.'

'Then he wants to make a statement,' said Tinkler. He glanced at his son, who looked even more uncomfortable. 'Perhaps the CPS will go easy on him if he helps.'

'Helps in what way?'

'Davie may have done something stupid, Inspector, you'll get no argument from me on that, but there's no way that he's going to be punished while that man gets away with it.'

'What man?' asked Harris.

'That feller whose wife the radio said were kill't last night.'

'George Fenchurch? What's he got to do with it?'

'Wouldn't you like to know?' Bill shot him a sly look. 'How would you fancy doing a deal, Chief Inspector?'

'I don't do deals.'

'You might want to do this one, Chief Inspector.'

Harris thought of the bodies being carried off the hillside following the plane crash.

'Do you know,' he said, 'you could well be right.'

Chapter twenty-four

'Sorry it's taken so long,' said Harris as he walked back into the interview room and sat down opposite Bill Tinkler and his son. 'This is complicated and Saturdays can be awkward, as I am sure you can appreciate.'

The inspector noticed the plastic cups on the table.

'Ah, I see that someone has brought you a cuppa,' he said. 'Good. Anyway, I have now talked to the duty Crown Prosecution lawyer.'

'And what did he say?' asked Bill. 'Are they going to drop the charges?'

'*She* was not very happy at the thought.'

'Why not? Did you tell her what I said?'

'I did, yes, but it's a Brian Blessed thing.' Harris chuckled at their bemused expressions. 'Long story. Anyway, I persuaded her to check with her boss and they've agreed to go ahead and offer you the deal.'

Father and son looked relieved.

'There are conditions, mind,' said Harris.

'So, what does Davie have to do?' asked Bill.

'If he is prepared to give a statement implicating George Fenchurch in the making of the film, the CPS will not proceed with any charges relating to the hoax call.

Same deal for the others. It turns out that Davie's girlfriend this morning accepted a similar deal in return for giving the National Crime Agency the name of the man who supplied the corpse.'

'Is she alright?' asked Davie. 'I've not heard from her since they took her away.'

'She is, but I'm not sure that you're her favourite person just now.' Harris gave the student a stern look. 'And you won't be mine if you come up with a load of flannel. I've stuck my neck out on this one.'

'I'll tell you what I know, Mister Harris.'

'You make sure you do.' Harris thought of Bob Crowther and the mountain rescue team battling their way across the windswept hill to rescue the girl, their eyes screwed up as the rain drove hard into their faces. 'There's plenty of people round here who would like to see you and your little pals hung out to dry for what you did. If the chopper had come down in that bad weather, we wouldn't be having this conversation. You can be sure of that. You'd have me to contend with for a start.'

Davie looked sick again. Harris gave a slight smile; job done, he thought. How he loved having a reputation.

'So, tell me what happened,' he said. 'George Fenchurch approached you, presumably? Where was this? The Cannes Film Festival, was it? Interrupt a conversation you were having with Quentin Tarantino, did he? And they say I don't do cultural references.'

Despite Davie Tinkler's anxiety, the student still managed a rueful smile.

'Not quite,' he said.

'Tell the Chief Inspector what you told me this morning,' said Bill, looking at his son. 'You were in the pub, weren't you?'

Davie nodded and a lock of lank black hair flopped across his eyes. He pushed it back into place.

'Yeah,' he said. 'I was with my girlfriend. Four or five weeks back it was. We were in The Royal Oak at Maunby,

159

having a quiet pint. Fenchurch, he was stood by the bar with a glass of soda water or something. He was watching us. I thought he was a perv or something.'

'Did you know him?' asked Harris.

'Na, never seen him before in my life.' Davie allowed himself another smile. 'He's not exactly my type of person. Bit uptight for me.'

'Bit uptight for everyone,' said Harris. 'Then what?'

'Well, he comes over and says that he'd heard that I make films and asks if I could make one for him. All very cloak and dagger, it was. He asked if we could talk about it in the car park where no one could hear.'

'Why did he want it doing? Did he say?'

'Said it was a joke. But it wasn't, Mister Harris. He didn't want it to be funny, said it had to be deadly serious.'

Davie was talking quickly now; Harris sensed that the young man was relieved to be unburdening himself of the truth at long last.

'He said that the film had to be real convincing, like. Said it had to make people believe that the mountain rescue blokes really had found that Graydon fellow up on the hills. And he said he wanted it quick.'

'Did he say why it had to be so convincing? Or why he wanted it done so quickly?'

'Said it wasn't none of our business.'

'And he was going to pay you?' asked Harris. 'How much?'

'Five grand between the three of us.'

Harris gave a low whistle.

'Yeah,' said Davie, 'for that kind of money, we weren't going to ask no questions. Buy a lot of cider, that would.'

'I guess it would,' replied the inspector. 'And when was he going to pay you? Once you'd made the film, I am guessing.'

'Yeah. When the fuss had died down. He said that if we told anyone that he was involved, he'd deny it and there'd be no money. We made up the story about doing it for our uni course just in case anyone asked.'

'And when you posted the film on YouTube? What happened next?'

'He was delighted,' said Davie. 'Said it was better than he could ever have imagined. And he was dead pleased when it got on Sky News. He said we'd done really well and that we'd earned our money.'

'Presumably, he was not as pleased when we revealed it as a hoax?'

'No, he was livid.' Davie frowned at the memory. 'He rang me up just after your lot said it was a fake. He really went off on one. Said he knew that you'd work it out eventually but didn't think it would be that quick. Said he thought he'd have more time.'

'That mention of time again,' murmured Harris. 'What do you think he meant by that?'

'Dunno, I was more worried about the money. He said he'd have to think about how much to pay us. Said it might not be the full five grand. He knew that we wouldn't dare complain to the police about it, the trouble we were already in. Besides, like he said, who would you lot believe, a respectable bloke like him or a bunch of scruffy students mucking about? His words.'

'He may well be right,' said Harris. 'So, you kept his name out of it when my officers came to see you.'

'Yeah. We thought that there was still a chance that he'd pay us when he'd cooled down a bit. Besides, even if he didn't, we reckoned we might get away with a telling off if anyone did trace it back to us. Never thought we'd get charged for a bit of nonsense like that.'

'It may have started out as a bit of nonsense,' said Harris, 'but I have this awful feeling that it cost an innocent woman her life.'

He pushed a piece of paper and a pen across the table.

'Write,' he said. 'Who knows, if it's good enough someone might turn it into a film.'

* * *

Perry St Martin was just about to go out when his mobile phone rang. He looked down at the read-out. Fenchurch, it said. He scowled, thought twice about taking the call, but eventually relented.

'What do you want?' he said.

'You didn't need to kill her,' replied Fenchurch's angry voice. St Martin could hear the emotion in his face. 'She didn't deserve that.'

'They didn't mean to – but if you play with the big boys, George...'

'Don't give me that!' snapped Fenchurch. 'I think the police may be onto me. Jack Harris kept looking at me funny last night. I think he knows what's been happening. Where's my money?'

'Where's the altimeter?'

'It's safe enough,' said Fenchurch. 'You didn't think I'd be stupid enough to keep it at my house for your goons to find, did you? You can have it when I get my money.'

'Why should I pay you?' sneered St Martin. 'She ain't going to need it now, is she?'

'How dare you...'

'Goodbye, George,' said St Martin. 'Don't contact me again.'

St Martin ended the call.

'I seem to be saying that a lot,' he murmured.

He looked round the villa and sighed.

'Time to move on again,' he said sadly and dialled another number.

Chapter twenty-five

The incident room at Levton Bridge Police Station was a hive of activity. Police officers made calls, received calls, scrolled down computer screens and compared notes. All was movement, apart from Scoot and Archie, who dozed next to one of the radiators. At the centre of the activity was Jack Harris, constantly pacing the room and relishing the buzz. The scene reminded him of his Manchester days and, despite his love of the hills and the slower pace of life that he so appreciated, the inspector was enjoying the thrill of a major investigation.

'Sir,' said one of the detectives, walking up to him. 'We've had a sighting of George Fenchurch's car. Couple of traffic officers.'

'Where?'

'M6 southbound. Heading into Staffordshire.'

'Did they stop him?'

'I am afraid not. By the time they had clicked who he was, he'd disappeared. Every car in the area is keeping a look-out for him, though. Where do you think he's heading?'

'Out of the country, I suspect,' said Harris grimly. 'Any luck on those airport checks?'

'He's well past Manchester so it's not going to be there. Gatwick say no one of that name is booked on any of their flights and we are waiting to hear from Heathrow and Stansted. Nothing from any of the ports yet.'

'Check private airfields as well. In case he plans to fly himself out.'

Another plainclothes officer approached, holding a couple of computer print-outs.

'The phone company came through,' he said. 'George Fenchurch has made several calls to the same mobile number over the past five weeks.'

'Any idea who it belongs to?' asked Harris.

'They can't tell us that, but their techies reckon it's someone living abroad somewhere. Spain, probably.'

'Makes sense,' said the inspector.

The officer hesitated. He looked uncomfortable.

'What's wrong?' asked Harris.

'It appears that George Fenchurch is not the only bad apple,' said the officer, his voice low so that only Harris could hear. 'See, the techies also managed to get hold of the outgoing calls from the Spanish phone.'

'Really? How did they do that?'

'They said it was better that we did not know. Anyway, there was a number on the list that I recognised. In fact, I had to ring it yesterday.'

'Yesterday?'

The officer took his smartphone from his pocket, clicked on the contacts list and held it up so that Harris could read it. The inspector's eyes widened.

'Are you sure?' he asked.

'I am afraid I am, sir. It would explain why they're always one step ahead of us, wouldn't it?'

'I am afraid it would.' The inspector's phone rang. 'Listen, keep this to yourself for the moment, will you? At least until I can work out what the hell is going on. And who I can trust.'

'Of course.'

Harris glanced down at his phone. The caller was Gallagher.

'Talking of trust,' said the inspector and smiled. He took the call. 'What you got, Matty lad?'

'The whole story,' said the sergeant.

Harris listened for a few minutes, gave a grunt of satisfaction and ended the call. He headed for the door.

'Right, I'm off to brief Curtis,' he said. 'Come and find me if anything else crops up, will you? And tell Staffordshire that I want Fenchurch. No fuck-ups.'

The inspector strode purposefully down the corridor and knocked on the commander's office door. Once the superintendent had given him a mug of tea, the inspector sat looking smug as Curtis stared dubiously across the desk at him.

'Are you sure you're right about this?' said Curtis. 'I mean, get it wrong and it's a PR disaster.'

'Now how did I know you were going to say that?' said Harris. 'But yes, I am right. About the main thrust of it anyway, there's a few details to fill in but we're getting there.'

'So, what do we know for certain?'

Harris glanced at the notepad on his knee.

'OK,' he said. 'This is from checks of bank records carried out by Jenny Armannsson. On February 13th, 1999, less than two months after the crash, George Fenchurch received a transfer into his bank account of £58,000, followed by another £42,000 six days later. A lot of money in those days. A lot of money now, for that matter.'

'Who was it from?'

'A company called J G Holdings.'

'What do we know about them?'

'Virtually nothing,' said Harris. 'Jenny thinks it was some kind of shell company. Whatever it was, it no longer exists. I suspect the name is a little joke. I think the J G is John Graydon.'

'So, he definitely wasn't on the plane?'

'I don't think he was, no. Unfortunately, the conspiracy theorists would appear to have been right on this occasion.'

'Just what we don't need. So, who got onto the aircraft?'

'Best guess? Two of them sacrificed the other one to let them get away with the money.'

'Nice people.' Curtis took a drink of coffee from his mug. He looked happier now that he was being presented with some answers after a week of frustration and confusion. 'And you think the payments to Fenchurch were to arrange the accident?'

'No, James Trewick's wife called Fenchurch a parasite. I think this is about good old-fashioned blackmail.'

'And Fenchurch was the blackmailer?'

'I reckon so. According to Margaret Trewick, her husband confessed what he'd done when Fenchurch went to interview him after the crash. Couldn't live with the guilt.'

'But Fenchurch kept it to himself?' said Curtis.

'I think he told Graydon that he'd make sure the report said pilot error if he was paid to keep quiet.'

'But if Trewick felt so guilty, why not go to the police anyway?'

'Because Fenchurch told him that not only would they jail him and throw away the key, it was likely that the families of those who died would sue him. Trewick faced seeing his wife and kids being thrown onto the street and he could not bear the thought. I tell you, George Fenchurch is a cruel and calculating man.'

'And you never did like him,' said Curtis.

'And I never did like him.'

* * *

166

Sitting in the incident room, Alison Butterfield ended yet another phone conversation, sighed and put the receiver down.

'This is hopeless,' she said to no one in particular.

The detective constable had been ringing nursing homes in the North West for three hours, persuading duty staff to contact their managers, arguing the point about patient confidentiality, waiting for calls-back that never came and, as she became increasingly irritable, threatening to charge people with obstructing a police investigation. All without turning up the information that Harris wanted.

What had made the experience worse was the fact that everyone else seemed to be enjoying what they were doing and all the talk of airports and traffic surveillance had made Alison Butterfield feel increasingly left-out. The exasperated detective ran her finger down the list on her desk, drew a line through the one she had just telephoned and picked up the phone again.

'Good afternoon,' she said. 'Is that Hill View Nursing Home? This is Detective Constable Butterfield at Levton Bridge Police Station. Can I speak to the duty manager, please?'

'I am afraid she's busy,' said a man's voice. 'Still doing the beds.'

'Tell her it's part of a murder inquiry.'

'Like I said...'

'Just tell her,' said Butterfield.

Ten minutes later, the detective constable slammed the phone down, said 'bingo' and headed at speed into the corridor in the direction of the commander's office.

* * *

The Staffordshire traffic officers were cruising in the inside lane of the southbound M6 in their unmarked vehicle when the car overtook them. The constable in the passenger seat read the registration number.

'That looks familiar,' he said. He checked the on-board computer. 'Yup. Blue Audi. That's the guy that they want up north for blackmail.'

'Best ring it in then,' said the driver.

* * *

'How come Fenchurch tried to blackmail Graydon a second time?' asked Curtis.

'His wife,' said Harris. 'When I was down in Stevenage, he said that she has to go into a nursing home – and they're not cheap.'

'Certainly aren't. Took most of my mother-in-law's savings. Enough to drive any man to crime.'

There was a knock on the door and Butterfield walked in, her face flushed with excitement.

'We've got him,' she said.

Noting the commander's bemused expression, Harris said, 'I had Constable Butterfield do some checking with nursing homes in the area. I am assuming that you found something?'

Butterfield nodded and referred to her notebook.

'Hill View Care Home, near Carlisle,' she said. 'George Fenchurch contacted them about his wife six weeks ago and they quoted a thousand pounds a week.'

Harris gave a low whistle.

'I told you,' said Curtis. 'My father-in-law had to sell their house.'

'And did Fenchurch take them up on their kind offer?' asked Harris, looking at Butterfield.

'He did, yes.' Butterfield glanced at her notebook again. 'She is booked in from the 12th of next month. Fenchurch told them that he needed a bit of time to get the money together.'

'And now we know how he planned to do it,' said Harris. 'Good work, Constable.'

'Will that be all?' asked Butterfield.

'I'm OK if you want to stay,' said Harris. 'You may learn something about what happens when a detective ignores his instincts.'

Curtis frowned but said nothing. Butterfield beamed and took a chair; she loved being involved in major inquiries and, having watched on enviously as other officers were allocated what she felt were the better assignments, now she was at the very heart of things. Her eyes gleamed.

Harris took another sip of his tea.

'The problem for George Fenchurch,' he said, resuming his story, 'was that the original money had all gone. Jenny's checks revealed that George and Elizabeth Fenchurch had expensive tastes before she fell ill. Three or four foreign holidays a year, the best resorts, the best hotels, first class flights, fancy restaurants.'

'And Graydon didn't fancy footing the bill second time around?' said Curtis.

'I reckon not. So, to focus his mind, Fenchurch gets the kids to make the film. Get everyone talking about the crash again. He knew he could rely on the conspiracy theorists to stir things up with the anniversary approaching. I think he was betting on Graydon getting panicky and paying up.'

There was another knock on the door and a uniformed officer walked in.

'Sorry to interrupt,' he said, 'but we've had Staffordshire on again. They've clocked Fenchurch's car, want to know if you want him stopped or tailed?'

'Stopped,' said Harris firmly.

'I'll tell them,' said the officer and left the room.

'One thing puzzles me,' said the commander. 'Who was the fraud squad's caller?'

'Fenchurch again, I reckon. When Graydon played hard-ball, I think Fenchurch wanted to increase the pressure and guessed that Air Traffic would ask him to help out if there was a new investigation.'

'But wouldn't that draw attention to himself?'

'So what if it did? He knew the investigation would come to the same conclusion, whoever carried it out. But Graydon didn't. When he still refused to pay up, Fenchurch tells him that he's got the altimeter – and condemns his own wife to death.

'So, what now?' asked Curtis.

'Well, I've always fancied a trip to the Cayman Islands…'

Chapter twenty-six

The Staffordshire Police motorway patrol vehicle continued to head south on the M6 at a steady pace, keeping at a discreet distance from the Audi so that George Fenchurch did not realise he was being followed. Noticing the traffic thinning out slightly ahead of them, the police driver glanced across at this fellow officer in the passenger seat.

'OK, let's do this,' he said. 'Their DCI will not be very pleased if we lose him again.'

'Sounds good to me.'

'Hang onto your hat then.'

The driver reached over, flicked on the blue lights and pressed his foot on the accelerator. The engine roared and Fenchurch looked in his rear-view mirror and noticed that the patrol car had moved into the outside lane and was approaching at speed. The Audi jolted forwards.

'He's running,' said the officer in the passenger seat.

The police car sped up as the Audi weaved in and out of the busy traffic. Cars swerved, horns blared, lights flashed and brake lights glowed red as Fenchurch tried desperately to escape from the pursuing vehicle. Noticing what has happening, a heavy goods vehicle lumbered into the middle lane and made as if to manoeuvre itself into the outside lane to block the Audi's progress. Fenchurch's brake lights glowed a vivid red as he slammed his foot onto the pedal and he momentarily slowed before pushing the accelerator down even harder and shooting past the lorry with inches to spare between the vehicle and the central reservation barriers.

Fenchurch glanced in his rear-view mirror again and the Audi's speed hit one hundred as he saw that the police vehicle had been held up by a slow-moving car despite repeatedly flashing its headlights for its driver to move out of the way. The Audi began to stretch away but, as the police car finally found a way through the traffic and once again narrowed the gap, Fenchurch noticed a sign for a turn-off. He pressed his foot down once more, taking the Audi up to a hundred and twenty, then as he approached the slip road, he wrenched hard on the steering wheel and the Audi veered across the lanes of traffic. More horns blared and more cars swerved as he left the motorway at high speed, his front wheel clipping the verge.

The Audi did not slow as it reached the roundabout at the top of the slip road and its brake lights did not show.

'He's not stopping!' cried the police driver.

The officers watched in horror as Fenchurch wrenched on the steering wheel again and, with a screeching of tyres, the Audi collided with a road sign, span round twice and careered into a tree. The vehicle came to a juddering halt on impact, with its horn blaring and smoke billowing from beneath its crumpled bonnet. Only seconds behind it, the police car came to a halt and the officers jumped out and ran towards the Audi. Acutely aware of the smell of petrol as it spilled out of the ruptured fuel tank, they tried to pull open the driver's door but it had dug itself deep into the grass and it took almost a minute to wrench it free.

Inside the vehicle, George Fenchurch was lying motionless, groaning, with blood pouring from a gaping head wound. The police driver looked at his colleague and shook his head in disbelief.

'He didn't stop,' he said. 'He just didn't stop.'

He gestured behind him at the road.

'No brake marks,' he said.

'An error of judgement?' asked his fellow officer.

The driver glanced back into the vehicle at the badly injured figure of George Fenchurch, his skin a deathly pale as the life ebbed away from him.

'Do you know,' he said, 'I am not sure that it was.'

* * *

Jack Harris was sitting in his office when Matty Gallagher walked into the room.

'You're back then,' said the inspector.

'Brilliant observation. That's why they made you a DCI and left me as a humble sergeant.'

'And don't you forget it, Matty lad. When did you get in?'

'A few minutes ago,' replied the sergeant. He held up a brown envelope. 'Clutching Margaret Trewick's statement in my sweaty little paw. I think she was glad to get things off her chest once she realised we had worked out what's been happening.'

'Good work.'

'It was the DI really. She's got the human touch has that woman.' Gallagher sat down and gave a weary sigh. 'Quite a day, all in all. I hear that Staffs got Fenchurch?'

'What's left of him. He ploughed his car into a road sign.'

'So, I heard. Someone said the traffic officers reckoned he did it deliberately.'

'The coward's way out,' said Harris. 'So much for the less robust ones.'

'What does that mean?'

'Something he said to me when we were in Stevenage.'

'He's still alive, apparently.'

'Yeah, but I'm not sure for how long. He's been taken to hospital in Stoke. Punctured lung, a load of broken ribs, damage to his spleen.' The inspector glanced up at the wall clock. 'He should be going into surgery about now.'

'I hope the bastard dies.'

'Not like you to let personal feelings intrude,' said Harris. 'I'm normally the one who does that.'

'Yeah, I know.' Gallagher thought for a few moments. 'It's something to do with the cruelty of it all, I think. I know that no one comes out of this well but what Fenchurch did, it's pernicious.'

'And bringing an aircraft down with all those innocent people on board wasn't?'

'Of course, it was. It's just...' Gallagher sought the right words. 'Those relatives of the crash victims we have been talking to over the past few days? I know they will never forget what happened but at least they had found a way to live with it. Then what happens? We turn up in our hobnail boots, making wild accusations that their loved ones might have been murdered. All without a shred of evidence and based on the actions of a man who believed it could never be proved. It's wicked. Stirs up all those memories.'

'They were already stirred up,' said Harris. He thought of the men who had died in the air crash in Belize, their crushed bodies, the twisted limbs, the lifeless eyes. His Captain. 'And you're wrong, none of them will have found a way to live with it. There will not be a day, not an hour in a day, when they do not think about what happened.'

'I suppose so.'

'Besides, what was the alternative? We had to investigate, didn't we?'

'Yes, but we only worked it out because Trewick got an attack of guilt on his deathbed. We were lucky. Without that, we would have been unable to prove anything, and Fenchurch knew it. He was quite prepared to see us toy with the relatives' emotions.'

'You know as well as anyone that our job is to follow the truth, wherever it takes us,' said Harris. 'And however many people end up being hurt in the process.'

'I guess,' said Gallagher. 'Yes, you're right. I'm just tired. Yeah, it's better that Fenchurch lives. Someone has to face the music.'

The inspector's desk phone rang. He picked up the receiver.

'How do you fancy kicking some doors in?' asked Leckie's voice at the other end.

'Always,' said Harris. 'And I am pretty sure that my esteemed sergeant will agree, the mood he's in. Are we picking them at random, Graham, or have you got somewhere in mind?'

'This is Manchester, not the cowboy country you run. No, one of our DCs on the south side of the city has just been on the blower. They think they've tracked down the guys who killed Elizabeth Fenchurch. No need to rush. They're in a pub, looks like they'll be there all night. We wondered if you fancied popping down to do the honours?'

'Would we ever,' said Harris.

He ended the call, stood up and reached for his coat.

'Come on, young fellow me lad,' he said to Gallagher. 'Time for you to run some of that energy off before bedtime. But we've got a little job to do first...'

Chapter twenty-seven

Shortly before 7pm, a weary Jenny Armannsson was sitting in her dimly lit office when the laptop pinged to herald the arrival of an e-mail. Noticing that the message had come from the security officer at one of the big banks, she leaned forward and clicked to open.

'At last,' she said.

Hi Jenny,

Sorry, it's been so long but we've been snowed under. Some mindless moron at the Nantwich branch took it upon himself to click on a porn link on his office computer and unleashed all holy hell. I can't move for naked Russians. Anyway, enough of my problems. I finally got to do some checking for you. Your DCI pal looks like he might be right on both counts. See attachments. Hope they help.

The detective inspector opened the attachments and scanned through the rows of figures.

'Jack Harris right again,' she said on reaching the bottom of the page. 'You really are something, my lad.'

Armannsson glanced up at the wall clock as there was a knock on the door.

'Bang on time,' she murmured. 'Come in!'

Danny Caulker entered the room.

'You wanted to see me,' he said.

'I did, yes, grab a seat, Danny.'

Caulker sat down.

'How'd it go with the chief?' he asked.

'Awkward.'

Caulker gave a knowing smile.

'I'm not surprised,' he said. 'It's been a fuck up from start to finish. Are you still my gaffer?'

'I am afraid not.'

Caulker tried to look sympathetic.

'Ah, that's a pity,' he said. 'But I guess you always suspected that the job was beyond you. Maybe in a few...'

'I didn't get sacked, Danny.'

'You didn't?' He looked worried.

'No, I didn't.' She gave him a look. 'So, you'll have to pay everyone back, won't you?'

'I don't know what...'

'I'm not stupid, Danny.' Her voice was cold. Clipped. Dangerous. 'I know that you've been running a book on me getting fired.'

'I can explain.'

'Yeah, so can I. Jack Harris is right, you're a small-minded misogynist.'

'Now hang on. Jack Harris has no...'

'But that's not why I wanted to see you.' Armannsson glanced over to the door as a grim-faced Jack Harris walked into the room, followed by a stern-looking Matty Gallagher.

'What the...?' said Caulker.

'The game's up, Danny,' said Harris.

Caulker looked at him uneasily.

'What do you mean?' he said.

Harris held up a computer print-out.

'Your phone calls to your little pal in Spain,' he said. 'Listed in black and white.'

Caulker went pale.

'And,' said Armannsson, turning her computer round so that the detective could see the figures ranged across the screen, 'your payments as well. What were they for, Danny? An inside track on our investigation? Naughty, naughty.'

Caulker stood up and headed for the door, only for Harris to block his way. For a moment or two, it looked as if Caulker would try to barge past him.

'Just try it, Danny,' said Harris. His voice was laden with menace. 'Because the way I feel about low-life like you, I would happily drop you where you stand.'

'And when you'd got up,' said Gallagher, 'I'd do the same thing, you little shit.'

Caulker slumped back into his chair and closed his eyes. Harris looked at Armannsson.

'Your arrest, I think, Detective Inspector,' he said. 'Something tells me that you could use it more than me.'

Chapter twenty-eight

It was shortly after eight when Harris, with Gallagher in the passenger seat, guided the Land Rover through Manchester's night-time streets. As the inspector looked out at the shadows cast on glistening, rain-swept pavements by the street lamps, memories came crowding in, as they always did, when his job took him back to the city. But although the inspector had fond recollections of much of his time in Manchester, the thought of his dogs now lying in the back of the vehicle reminded him that life in the valley was preferable. The occasional return visit would suffice. Besides, the encounter with Danny Caulker had left a bitter taste in his mouth.

Sitting beside him, Matty Gallagher was just enjoying being in a city again. Harris glanced across at him.

'I'm glad you're here,' said the inspector with the slightest of smiles. 'Nice to know who you can trust.'

'Sentimental bastard,' said Gallagher.

Eventually, Harris turned into a derelict terraced back street on the south side of Manchester and parked outside a dilapidated corner shop whose peeling paint and boarded up windows defaced by graffiti suggested that it had long since closed down. The detectives got out and surveyed the scene. A series of police vans with their headlights extinguished were lined up along the street and officers in riot gear were gathered in groups, chatting, some smoking, some looking intently at their smartphones. A faint, ironic cheer went up when the inspector alighted from the Land Rover.

'Friends of yours?' said Gallagher.

'Some of them.'

'Only some of them?'

'You know how it is,' said Harris.

Gallagher gave a slight smile but said nothing. He knew exactly how it was with Jack Harris. The detectives walked over to where Leckie was standing by one of the vans. Harris and Leckie shook hands then Leckie did the same with Gallagher. It was a warm handshake; Leckie had grown to like and respect the sergeant. Gallagher was good for Harris, he had decided. Besides, any friend of Jack Harris…

'Did you sort that other thing?' asked Leckie.

'I am afraid so,' said Harris.

'Nasty business. Did he try to get out of it?'

'Would you?'

Leckie looked at Harris's muscular frame.

'No,' he said. 'No, I wouldn't.'

'What have we got then?' asked Harris. He gestured to the vans. 'And why all the cavalry?'

'They're in a pub a few streets down,' said Leckie. 'Big do. Birthday bash. Proper gangland who's who, it is. You'll recognise plenty of faces when you get in there.'

'They're going to give us trouble?' The inspector's eyed gleamed. 'Not that I would object, of course. The mood I'm in…'

'You rural types coming into our city with your troublemaking ways,' said Leckie with a smile. 'But, no, we should be alright. Our informant assured us that there'd be no trouble when we lifted the lads. Ordinarily I would put my head out of the window if a crim told me it was raining but this time I believe them.'

Leckie gave his friend a sly look.

'For some reason,' he said, 'they don't want you to spend a minute longer in Manchester than you have to.'

'Nice to be loved,' said Harris. 'Any idea who your informant is?'

'Anonymous call but I've got a pretty good idea. He's just the errand boy, though. Usual story. Our lot were asking too many questions, and the crims were less than impressed that you were involved as well, so they gave up these two jokers to persuade us to go away.'

'And who are we looking for exactly?' asked Gallagher.

'A right couple of darlings,' said Leckie. 'One Malky Stabler – Malks to his friends – and Jimmy Myles. Bit of a hothead is Jimmy. I am guessing that he's the one who beat up your old dear.'

'Do we know much else about them?' asked Harris.

'They're not exactly big league, they hang around the periphery mainly. Couple of wannabees. You'll not know them, I don't think, Hawk. Too far down the food chain when you were here. Still are.'

'Certainly, neither name rings a bell,' said Harris. 'Is your caller sure they're our guys?'

'He's adamant. Reckons they were associates of Perry St Martin and Edward Gough.'

'Miriam Jacques' dodgy visitors, I've no doubt,' said Harris. Noticing the others looking perplexed, he added, 'I think that they used to hang around John Graydon's offices.'

'Could well be,' said Leckie. 'Anyway, I checked our records – they've both got long rap sheets, including a couple of aggravated burglaries. Jimmy gave another old woman a slap in one of them, broke her jaw, which would fit with your attack on Elizabeth Fenchurch.'

'They sound delightful,' said Gallagher.

'Couple of pests,' said Leckie. 'Dangerous ones, at that. You're doing us a favour taking them away.'

A uniformed inspector wearing riot gear walked over to them. He nodded at Harris.

'Long time, no see, Jack,' said the officer. 'Still walking the dogs?'

'Hello, Barrie,' replied Harris. He glanced across at his Land Rover. 'Yeah, they're in the back.'

'Thought they might be,' said the uniformed officer. 'We good to go then? The guys are getting restless. There's only so much Candy Crush a person can take.'

Harris looked bewildered.

'It's a game,' said Gallagher. He looked at the uniformed officer. 'The governor does not do cultural references.'

'Yeah, I forgot.' The uniformed inspector grinned. 'Still no telly?'

'Still no telly,' said Gallagher.

The uniformed officer looked at Harris.

'So, are we OK to go in then?' he asked.

'Yeah, fine,' said the detective.

'Well, you just behave yourself when we do,' said the uniformed inspector. 'None of your old tricks.'

Gallagher looked quizzically at Harris.

'It's a long story,' said Harris.

'They all are,' said Leckie.

The uniformed officer gave a signal, the raiding teams clambered into the vehicles, the headlights came on and the vans started to move. Harris and Gallagher returned to the Land Rover and followed them. After a couple of minutes, the vans turned into another rundown street and pulled to a halt outside a pub. The riot teams disembarked and assembled quietly and efficiently. Seconds later, the teams burst into the hostelry. As the Levton Bridge detectives followed them in, they walked into a silent scene, the drinkers watching as the riot officers lined up in front of the door. No one moved. No one spoke.

Harris surveyed the room for a few moments. Just as Leckie had promised, there were some familiar figures, and the inspector smiled slightly as he noticed the uneasy flickers of recognition on a number of faces. He knew that there were plenty of criminals who had been delighted when he left the city for pastures north; Leckie had told him after he left that there was the largest party that one of the local public houses had ever seen. However, Harris did not have much time to savour the moment because a shaven-headed man in his fifties walked up to him. They stood and eyeballed each other for a couple of moments.

'I take it you've been told about the deal?' said the gang leader. 'You fuck off out of Manchester when you've got them?'

'When we're done, yes,' said Harris.

'And when will that be?'

'When we're done,' said the detective. He gave the man a hard look. 'And only then. Where are they?'

The gang leader nodded towards the back of the lounge where two men had slipped through the rear door. Harris glanced across at the uniformed inspector.

'Be my guest,' said the officer with an exaggerated wave of the hand. 'Just remember what I said.'

Harris gestured to Gallagher and they walked across the bar and pushed their way through the door. Once through, they found themselves in a dark and dingy corridor that smelled of mouldy carpets and stale urine.

'Delightful,' said Gallagher.

'All pot plants and air fresheners in Da Smoke, is it?' said Harris.

Gallagher chuckled and the detectives walked to the far end and into the Gents only to find the room empty. Without speaking, they walked back into the corridor, Harris nodded and they pushed their way into the female lavatories. The doors to two of the cubicles were closed. Harris looked at his sergeant and Gallagher launched himself at the first door, which gave way with a splintering of wood to reveal a cowering man. As Gallagher stepped back, Harris delivered a hefty kick to the second door, which came off one of its hinges and swung open to reveal the second man, a terrified expression on his face.

Harris stepped back and gave the two men a disarming smile.

'Hello, ladies,' he said. 'Beaten up any defenceless pensioners lately?'

'We didn't mean to kill her,' said Malky Stabler as Gallagher hauled him out of the cubicle. 'It was an accident.'

'You can tell it to the judge,' said Harris. He reached forward and hauled Jimmy Myles out by his shirt collar. 'But I don't reckon he'll believe you.'

The detectives led the two men out into the lounge, watched in silence by the assembled drinkers. At the door, Harris turned round and searched the sea of faces for the gang leader who had confronted him. Spotting him, the detective gave a slight smile.

'Till next time,' he said.

The man gave him a dirty look but said nothing. A minute later, the detectives were back in the street, watching as a couple of uniformed officers loaded the arrested men into one of the vans.

'Just like old times, eh?' said Leckie.

'Yeah,' said Harris. 'But give me a fishing trip any day, Graham.'

'You'll not get any argument from me, old son.'

The detectives had just climbed into the Land Rover when the inspector's smartphone rang and he took the call.

'Gillian,' he said. 'Yeah, got them both. Na, good as gold. GMP are going to keep them in for us.'

'Did they cough to it?' asked the detective inspector.

'Tried to say it was an accident but we'll let the CPS sort that one out. GMP are going to bring them up tomorrow morning for us.'

'You staying down there overnight then?'

'Yeah. If only to piss off all the people who want to see the back of me. Any other news?'

'That's why I am ringing, I am afraid' said Roberts. 'I have just had a call from the hospital in Stoke. George Fenchurch is dead.'

Harris ended the call and looked at Gallagher. The sergeant noted the inspector's expression.

'Fenchurch?' he asked.

'I am afraid so, Matty lad.'

'So it was all for nothing,' said the sergeant in a flat voice. He thought of the grief he had encountered in recent days. 'All that suffering and Trewick and Fenchurch are dead and the real perpetrators have got away with it again.'

'They can't run for ever.'

'Can't they?' asked Gallagher sourly. 'They've managed it for twenty years.'

'Well, this time I have this sneaking feeling that things will be different.'

Gallagher nodded in the direction of the police vans.

'You're thinking that Stabler and his little pal will give them up?' he asked. 'I can't see that. Nor Danny Caulker.'

'Not sure they will, Matty lad. No, I am thinking of someone else. Something Jenny told me after we'd lifted Caulker. Forgot to mention it amid all the excitement.'

Becoming aware of someone standing nearby, the inspector turned to see Armannsson in front of one of the vans.

'Hello, Jack.' She gave him a half-smile. 'Heard you might be staying the night in Manchester.'

'I'll get my coat,' said Gallagher.

Chapter twenty-nine

Thirty-six hours later, Jack Harris parked the Land Rover outside Miriam Jacques' house. She stood in the living room window and watched in silence as the inspector and Jenny Armannsson got out of the vehicle. Once the front doorbell had rung, Miriam waited for a few moments, leaning against the wall with her eyes closed.

'No,' said Miriam quietly. 'No, please God, no.'

The bell rang again.

'Miriam, open the door,' said Harris. His voice was harsh. 'I have a warrant to search your house.'

Miriam was filled with an overwhelming desire to run. She looked down the hall, at the paintings and the antiques, and tears glistened in her eyes at the thought of leaving it all behind.

There was a loud pounding on the door.

'Miriam!' shouted Harris.

She sighed and opened the door.

'Hello, Miriam,' said the inspector. 'I don't believe you have met DI Armannsson from Greater Manchester Police Fraud Squad. She's looking forward to our little chat. Can we come in?'

'I wondered when you'd come,' said Miriam, standing aside to let them into the hallway. 'Am I under arrest?'

'Not yet,' said Harris. 'But I imagine you will be soon. Depends how much you help us.'

Miriam ushered the detectives into the living room. Harris wandered over to the window and stared out at the new 4x4 parked in the drive. Armannsson sat down in one of the armchairs and studied the expensive paintings and ornaments.

'Nice,' she said. 'Were they paid for by John Graydon?'

Miriam did not reply but sat down on another armchair and eyed the detectives nervously.

'There's no point denying it,' said Armannsson. She thought of the email she had a received from the security officer. 'Your bank confirmed the payments.'

Armannsson took a notebook out of her jacket pocket and flipped through to the right page. She ran a finger down the column of figures, her lips moving as she added up the total.

'Fifty-seven and a half thousand in all,' she said. 'Nine payments in the year following the plane crash. That's a lot of hush money, Miriam.'

'I can explain.'

'So can I,' said Harris. He turned back into the room. 'See, the phone company has traced your recent calls to someone in Spain.'

Miriam closed her eyes.

'Would you like to know what we think?' said Harris. He sat down on the sofa. 'We think you were calling Graydon or one his pals. Tipping him off that we had come to see you. Are we right?'

Miriam nodded.

'Perry St Martin,' she said.

'And the payments twenty years ago were for what?' asked Armannsson.

'To make sure I told no one about the fraud. I helped them move some of the money. But I did not know anything about the plane crash being deliberate. You have to believe me.'

Miriam started to cry and Armannsson handed her a tissue. Once Miriam had recovered her composure, she turned dark eyes on the detectives.

'What will happen to me?' Her voice was barely audible.

'As it stands, you are in this up to your neck,' said Harris. 'However, were you point us in the direction of Perry St Martin…'

'Oh, no,' she exclaimed, 'I could not do that! He'd kill me. I'm not stupid. I saw on the news what happened to George Fenchurch and his wife. I don't want it happening to me.'

'In which case,' said Harris and he looked at Armannsson for confirmation, 'I suspect that you will be charged with fraud.'

Armannsson nodded.

'And does that mean that I will go to jail?' asked Miriam fearfully. 'For how long?'

'Up to ten years,' said Armannsson.

Miriam stared at her in horror.

'No,' she said. 'No!'

'But,' said Harris, leaning forward in his seat, 'were you to help us we could put a word in. Who knows, you might even get a suspended sentence.'

Chapter thirty

The first buds were on the trees when Jack Harris drove his Land Rover out of Levton Bridge and turned the vehicle south towards the motorway. Shortly after 2pm, he pulled up outside the main terminal of Manchester Airport where Jenny Armannsson was standing, waiting for him. She waved and Harris got out of the vehicle and gave her the lightest of kisses on the cheek.

'Ready?' he said.

'Yes.' She nodded to the Land Rover. 'But they won't let you leave it there, Jack.'

Harris said nothing and walked through the main entrance. Armannsson shrugged and the detectives headed into the arrivals hall where they stood and watched as the passengers streamed towards them, having disembarked from the Madrid flight. As the crowd thinned out, two officers wearing the uniform of the Spanish Police emerged, one of them handcuffed to a tall, unshaven man. Harris held up a hand and the officers guided Perry St Martin towards them. St Martin glared balefully at Harris and silently mouthed a profanity.

'Now, now, Perry,' said Harris. 'That's no way to behave, is it now?'

'DCI Harris?' said the officer handcuffed to the prisoner.

'The very same. You must be Inspector Ramos?'

Ramos nodded and gestured to the prisoner.

'And this,' he said, 'is all yours. And you're welcome to him.'

Harris looked intently at St Martin.

'Welcome home, Perry,' said the inspector. He gave a half smile. 'Did you have a nice flight? No problems?'

'Fuck off.'

'Language, language,' said Harris. He glanced at Jenny. 'See, you, me and DI Armannsson here have got so much to talk about over the next few days and we don't want to get off on the wrong foot, do we? For a start, we are rather hoping that you can point us in the direction of John Graydon.'

'Who?'

'Ah, well,' said Harris affably. He glanced at Armannsson. 'It looks like a couple of weeks in the Cayman Islands, after all. It's just a question of which of our esteemed chief constables will foot the bill.'

* * *

The following week, Bob Crowther, Jack Harris and the rest of the mountain rescue team were making their way carefully, and with some difficulty, down a slippery wooded hillside as the Spring rain drove hard and cold into their faces. It was just after lunchtime and they were heading for a young hiker who had tripped and broken his ankle while walking alone in the hills. It was three hours since he had called in and the team was eager to reach him as soon as possible. Spring it may be, warm it was not.

As they entered a narrow gulley, and as the rain started to sweep even harder across the hillside, one of the rescuers saw Scoot pawing at the ground. After looking closer, the man pointed to the ground and cried out excitedly. Running over to him, Crowther and Harris looked down in amazement at a series of weathered bones which were largely concealed by bracken.

'Not again,' said Crowther. He glanced round at the others. 'No one's filming us, are they?'

'Not this time,' said Harris. He crouched down beside the bones and gently move aside the fronds of bracken. 'No, these look genuine to me, Bob.'

The inspector reached out to touch them.

'Yup, they're real alright,' he said.

'Passenger Eleven?' said Crowther.

'I would have said so.' Harris looked at the marks gouged out by a large stone that had become dislodged and rolled down the slope before coming to rest in a stream. 'I suspect that was why the searchers did not find him first time around. It must have hidden him from view.'

Crowther nodded. The inspector noticed a bedraggled passport lying nearby. He walked over and picked it up. Opening it, and carefully cupping the document to prevent it crumbling in his hands, he could just about make out the remnants of a faded photograph depicting a short-haired man and the faint letters 'J', 'ra' and 'n'.

'John Graydon?' asked Crowther, walking across to peer over the inspector's shoulder.

'It'll bugger up my trip to the Cayman Islands with young Jenny Armannsson if it is.'

'Here!' Mike Ganton, who had been searching the area, bent down and held up a tattered drivers' licence which he carried carefully over to Harris. 'Careful, Hawk, it's falling to pieces.'

The inspector peered closely at the document and could just make out the letters 'dw' and 'gh'.

'Edward Gough,' said the inspector quietly. 'I'd lay money on this being the body of Edward Gough.'

'The fall guy,' said Crowther and gave a sly grin.

The rest of the team laughed but Crowther noticed that Harris had not. The rescue team leader patted his friend on the shoulder.

'Maybe Matty Gallagher's right,' he said. 'There's still work to do on your sense of humour.'

* * *

At the same time as the rescuers were discovering the remains of Edward Gough, Gallagher was sitting in the CID squad room at Levton Bridge Police Station, staring thoughtfully at the large gift-wrapped bottle of whisky standing on his desk. He opened the accompanying card and read the message again.

'That's nice,' asked Roberts. She walked over to him. 'One of your fans?'

'Something like that. It was left at the front desk twenty minutes ago.'

'Who by?'

'Patricia Malahide,' said the sergeant.

'What does the card say?'

'Thank you,' said Gallagher. He handed her the card. 'It says thank you.'

'But for what? Clearing her husband's name or securing all that compensation she's going to get?'

Gallagher fished a couple of glasses out of his desk drawer.

'Now there's a question,' he said.

And he reached for the bottle.

THE END

List of Characters

Levton Bridge Police:

Superintendent Philip Curtis – divisional commander
Detective Chief Inspector Jack Harris
Detective Inspector Gillian Roberts
Detective Sergeant Matty Gallagher
Detective Constable Alison Butterfield
Detective Constable Alistair Marshall

Other police officers:

Detective Inspector Jenny Armannsson, Head of Greater Manchester Police Fraud Squad
Detective Constable Danny Caulker, Greater Manchester Police Fraud Squad
Barrie – Greater Manchester Police uniformed inspector
PC Graham Leckie – intelligence officer with Greater Manchester Police

Other characters:

Anne – student
Beth – forensics officer
Bob Crowther – Head of Levton Bridge Mountain Rescue Team
Doc – Home Office pathologist
George Fenchurch – air accident investigator
Mike Ganton – Deputy Head of Levton Bridge Mountain Rescue Team
Edward Gough – businessman
Julie Gallagher – a nurse and Matty's wife
John Graydon – businessman
Tom Hawley – student
Len Howlett – former owner of aviation charter company Howletts
Miriam Jacques – a former secretary with John Graydon's company
Ray Malahide – pilot
Patricia Malahide – his wife
Laura Mayhew - Edward Gough's sister
Inspector Ramos – Spanish policeman
Jimmy Myles – criminal
Perry St Martin – businessman
Malky Stabler – criminal
James Trewick – former mechanic with Howletts
Margaret Trewick – his wife
Davie Tinkler – a student
Bill Tinkler – his father

If you enjoyed this book, please let others know by leaving a quick review on Amazon. Also, if you spot anything untoward in the paperback, get in touch. We strive for the best quality and appreciate reader feedback.

editor@thebookfolks.com

www.thebookfolks.com

Made in the USA
Lexington, KY
08 June 2019